GRUMPY OLD MEN

GRUMPY

New Year,

DAVID QUANTICK

OLD MEN

Same Old Crap

HarperCollins*Publishers*

HarperCollins*Publishers*
77–85 Fulham Palace Road,
Hammersmith, London W6 8JB

The web address is www.harpercollins.co.uk

First published by HarperCollins*Publishers* 2007
1

A catalogue record for this book
is available from the British Library

ISBN 0-00-724333-2
ISBN-13 978-0-00-724333-4

Printed and bound in Great Britain by
Clays Ltd, St Ives plc

Picture acknowledgements: p11 © Christopher Furlong/Getty Images;
p15 © ColumbiaTriStar/Getty Images; p21, 46 © Harry Todd/Getty Images;
p32 © Silver Screen Collection/Getty Images; p42 © Hulton Archive/Stringer/Getty
Images; p49 © Bruno Vincent/Staff/Getty Images; p53 © Dave Hogan/Getty Images;
p55 © John Kobal Foundation/Getty Images; p58 © Hulton Archive/Getty Images;
p69 © Hola Images/Getty Images; p74 © PM/Getty Images; p78 © Terry
O'Neill/Getty Images; p79 © John Stanton/Getty Images; p88, 139 © Chris
Ware/Getty Images; p98 © Lambert/Getty Images; p107 © Stacey/Getty Images;
p111 © Henry Groskinsky/Getty Images; p130 © Fox Photos/Getty Images;
p133, 147, 155 © AFP/Getty Images; p135 © Matt Cardy/Getty Images;
P149 © Ron Chapple/Getty Images; p152, 166, 176, 180 © Getty Images;
p159 © Ralph Morse/Getty Images

CONTENTS

INTRODUCTION

There used to be a huge piece of graffiti somewhere in London (this was years ago when graffiti was actual words and sentences, not someone's name spelt wrong in six different colours) that said, in huge wobbly letters, 'MODERN LIFE IS RUBBISH'. Now there are two things here. One is that years later a pop group stole that slogan for an album title, which is just typical. Get your own ideas, poppy boys! And the other is slightly more profound. That graffiti was sprayed up over twenty-five years ago. So if modern life was rubbish then, think how much more rubbish it is now.

Because the times, as Bob Dylan told us much to our huge surprise, are a-changing. They are, in fact, a-getting worse. And all the nice new modern things that are supposed to make our lives easier are almost certainly making it worse. Take work. You may remember a while ago some nonsense about 'the paperless office'. The idea was that when we all had computers and modems and wireless and so on, we'd no longer be printing documents and sending faxes and we'd manage without paper. And yet there seems to be more paper in offices than ever. Similarly, email. Does it speed up the pace of work life? It might, if we didn't spend all day deleting spam and replying to idiots who want to know if we went to school with them, and looking at web groups online where someone has sent you an important message and that message turns out to be 'Andrew is thinking of making himself a cup of tea'.

Modern life is more and more rubbish. And as it gets worse, men become more and more grumpy. The age limit for grumpiness seems to have been lowered, too. Grumpiness is no longer the preserve of the over-forties, or even the over-thirties. There are grumpy old men around who are barely out of their teens. And it's getting grumpier out there. All teenagers are permanently grumpy anyway; and ninety per cent of primary-school children are officially fed-up. As life gets worse, grumpiness looks more and more like the only sensible option.

There's never been a better time to be grumpy.

PEOPLE

PEOPLE WHO SAY, 'I JUST EAT WHAT I WANT ALL THE TIME AND I NEVER PUT ON ANY WEIGHT, I DON'T KNOW WHY'

~

Because after you've finished eating, you go to the toilet and throw up, that's why. You puking liar.

PEOPLE WHO DRESS YOUNG

~

Time was, you dressed like what you was. If you were a baby, you favoured some swaddling. Toddlers seemed keen to dress as miniature fops. Infants wore uniform until they left school. And then you were a man and you dressed as a man. This lasted you for bloody ages until you went to the clothes shop and said, through clacking false teeth and wispy nicotine-stained moustache, 'I am now an old man. Can I have my old man clothes, please?' And they would kit you out in flat cap, weskit, pipe and tweed jacket with leather elbow patches.

No more, alas, no more. These days you can dress up as what you like, when you like, until you drop dead. And what this means in practice is that everyone dresses young. See the octogenarian pop star in his baseball boots and Camden Market T-shirt! Observe the ageing accountant in his chinos and distressed jacket! Look at the Chelsea Pensioner dressed (because he's a bit behind with the fashions) like a member of All Saints, freshly back from a rave in the Gulf.

Nobody has seen fit to reverse this notion. Apart from the odd prawn who likes to dress up as a fogey just to make sure that they never have sex again, young people do not for the most part want to look like old people. Yet now they do, because the old people are all dressed as them. It's a paradox! How will we be able to tell the young people from the old people? Oh yeah, that's right. The old people will be the ones with the wrinkly skin and the back problems. And they'll also be the ones who can afford the trendy designer clothes, ha ha.

PEOPLE WHO GET ANNOYED WHEN ASKED TO PUT THEIR SHIRTS BACK ON
∾

Look around this pub, café or bar! Is anyone else not wearing a shirt? No! Has anyone said, 'Hey! Nice back! The acne scars blend in with the unsunscreened flaky skin!' Again, no! So put your shirt on, monkey boy!

LADS
∾

Thankfully we no longer have 'ladettes' (did we ever, really? Were they just made up, those girls drinking pints of lager and pretending to enjoy table football?) but we still have lads. God, do we have lads. The male ability to not grow up is so remarkable and logic-defying that one day Richard Dawkins will hear of it and throw his arms up in the air saying, 'All right! I give up! This is so mental that surely a higher power is behind it. Wow! There's a Power Rangers movie!'

Lads as a concept is a broad church (or, as Richard Dawkins would say, a broad brick building with pictures of dead imaginary people in the windows). It developed from your wartime mockers, brave but normal blokes who sank a tin mug of char before having a go at Jerry. The naughtiest thing these lads ever did was go to a bint in Cairo and pretend to have it off to save face.

There are bonny lads and stable lads and jack the lads and all sorts of lads whom nowadays we would just call 'teenagers', except teenagers can't clean a horse or make a fire or spell 'ant'. There are lads who are your mates, like in a beer advert, who sit in pubs and thump one another on the shoulder and are secretly in love with each other but not in a gay way.

But generally, when we think of 'lads' these days we think as the pensioner coming home late at night does – of white youths (because these days 'youths' is a word reserved solely for Asian or Afro-

Caribbean lads, as though white kids were never really young) heading towards him in hooded tops, carrying cans of Stronge Brew and doing that weird and no-way gay thing where they keep whacking each other and laughing, and they walk with a strange bendy gait so their legs look like brackets with a drink problem, and they're possibly harmless, but you'd better not stare at them, and while they're probably quite nice really (although you don't know it, three of them are at stage school), one of them could well be dangerously mental, so you step aside even though you've got the right of way.

Those lads.

LADS 2
∽

A nd let's not forget (would that we could) posh lads. It sounds like an oxymoron but there is such a thing as a posh lad. He certainly

'The male ability to not grow up is so remarkable and logic-defying that one day Richard Dawkins will hear of it and throw his arms up in the air saying, "All right! I give up!"'

thinks that he and his mates are lads. You can tell this because whenever a posh lad is walking down the street and he is more than a centimetre behind them, he always shouts, 'Lads! Wait up!' in a sort of strangled, where-are-my-balls kind of voice (note also the phrase 'Wait up!', which posh lad believes is some sort of cool slang).

Posh lads resemble normal lads in one way only: they are of the male gender. But there is no other kind of lad that wears a blazer to the pub, favours collarless shirts, often in a pastel shade, has either no chin or a chin the size of the *Tirpitz*, lips like sliced gherkins, the complexion of some brand-new ham, and the voice of a recently neutered earl.

All right, two ways: when they get hammered their manners are disgusting and they break stuff. Oh well. At least we don't have to till their sodding fields any more.

WAGs

The best example that there be of celebrity culture in action. Millions of years ago there were no famous wives of footballers. There were certainly no well-known girlfriends. History books may record the goal-scoring performance of H.K. Whittle (Woolwich Arsenal, 1931–1936) but of Mrs H.K. Whittle we know nothing. And the notion that Mrs H.K. Whittle would be photographed arriving at Hendon Aerodrome with 45 trunks full of Chanel dresses would have been considered absurd. Not to mention the idea that Mrs H.K. Whittle would be given her own show on the wireless, in which she and some other wives, including Mrs John Hemsley, Mrs G. Brill (Plymouth Argyle) and Mrs A.L.B. Cottersley would be placed in charge of two rival wool shops, the one to be named Hemsley Brill and Cottersley, the other to be named Quality

> 'There should be an exam for becoming famous. Although, thinking about it, it probably ought not to be a very difficult exam.'

Woollen Products of Neasden, with the aim being to discern which of the two teams were best, would be most common.

And yet such is life nowadays. Merely marrying or even having it off or sometimes just kissing a footballer is enough to make you famous nowadays, as though celebrity could be passed on through DNA (if that was the case, there would be an awful lot of pole-dancers and barmaids who'd become celebrities out there).

There should be an exam for becoming famous. Although, thinking about it, it probably ought not to be a very difficult exam.

PR PEOPLE

∾

Like marketing only even more useless (see 'MARKETING'). PRs do two jobs. One is phoning people up and begging them to write about some living soupstain who wants to be famous. They live their lives on the brimming edge of despair, hoping and praying that just one hack, somewhere, will be stupid or bribable enough to write about their act who, let's not forget, wouldn't need any PR if they were any good in the first place.

Astonishingly, some of their charges do make it and become stars. At this point they tire of fame and weary of success, unless they can get some more money from being famous and successful. So the PR has a new task, one utterly contradictory to their other task. The second job that PRs do is trying to prevent people writing about their acts. They block access, they deny quotes, they spread mystery. This is partly to make their stars look more charismatic and interesting, and partly because their client has just become addicted to valium dissolved in Coke Zero (see COKE ZERO) and has shaved their eyebrows off and gone to live in a seagull colony.

FAMOUS DEAD PEOPLE

∾

The overwhelming weight of the past or what? It's bad enough we have to deal with all the living celebrities without having to take note of everyone who went before. Scarcely an hour goes by without somebody unveiling a monument or a blue plaque to some minor non-entity of the past. It's as though every human being who had some tiny claim to fame has been listed like a historic building, and so, like a historic building, cannot be knocked down or removed from the public consciousness.

The internet (see THE INTERNET) contributes to this as well, with websites and nostalgia groups and obsessive research, all devoted to someone who co-hosted a moderately unsuccessful radio show in the late 1990s, or who once played bass guitar on an album by someone who never had a hit, or who wrote a novel that a film which didn't do very well was based on.

It's important to note and to pay respects to those who have gone on before us, but please! Does that have to mean everyone? We've got enough on our plate reading the complete works of Shakespeare and listening to everything Beethoven did without having to nod approvingly at the excellent work done by the man who drew Captain Soldier in *Warface!* magazine or the lady who would have introduced orchids to Lancashire only she had a cold.

KNIGHTS
∾

In days of old, when men were bold, and cash for questions wasn't invented, there was only one qualification for knighthood. You had to be really good at killing people. Oh, and you had to own a horse. But that was about it, really. It made sense.

'Hello, Alan, where have you been?'

'Sorry, your Majesty, I've been out killing people. Templars and that.'

'Well, why didn't you say so? Arise, Sir Gimblenore.'

'Oh! Ta.'

These days, you don't get a knighthood for killing people (although certain sections of the popular press would beg to differ, ahem, ahem (see POSH TABLOIDS)). You get one for things like helping the government when it's broke, or for having been on the *South Bank Show*, or for being good at acting, or for being a rock singer who hasn't died yet.

'In days of old … there was only one qualification for knighthood. You had to be really good at killing people.'

Which is a pity. They really ought to turn the clock back on this. Just to see 'Sir' Mick Jagger hurtling along on a horse, waving a wobbly lance, trying to spear 'Sir' Alan Sugar. They could sell tickets. They'd make a fortune.

PEERS
∾

Rubbish. It's one thing to see Lord Bugglesbath standing there, 90 years old in his stockinged feet and burbling on about rights of eschovy and mantraison in the voice of a broken budgerigar, because that's heritage. Lord Bugglesbath and his mates are kept in the House of Lords for their own protection, in case they go for a walk down a busy street and get run over by the twenty-first century.

But your modern peers are no good whatsoever. They sit there, in suits from M&S, wishing they hadn't been kicked off the board of their companies, wondering how much an ermine robe costs, and every so often going, 'I'm a lord. How the hell did that happen?'

Not to be encouraged. Oh, and that thing where if you're called Dennis Surname and they ask you to be a life peer and tell you to pick a title? Don't call yourself Lord Surname! Use your imagination! You could be called anything you want to be! Lord Axes! Lord Mince Warriors! Lord Lord! Anything. You dull lord, you.

PEOPLE WHO'VE GONE CLASSICAL

ᕫ

Doesn't go the other way much, does it? Apart from that bloke who did the *South Bank Show* music and some ill-advised John Williams records, most classical musicians tend to eschew the world of pop, probably because they know they'd be no good at it. They know that purely because you can play all the notes in the world and read music and everything doesn't actually mean that you'll be good at just whacking a guitar or a keyboard and making onky noises all the live-long day. (Although this doesn't apply to the Vanessa-Maes of this world, who know all this and don't care, probably because they are sadists and like the idea of taking a perfectly innocent bit of Bach, tying it to a wall and throwing drums at it.)

But Johnny and Jane Pop Singer have no such compunction. Blithely unaware that what they do is a perfectly valid art form and who cares if it isn't, it's hugely entertaining and they're good at it, they get delusions of something and before you know it, they're attempting a form which is just similar enough to what they're already doing to not worry them (see PEOPLE WHO ARE FAMOUS FOR ONE THING AND THEN GO AND DO ANOTHER THING). 'Ooh, a lute,' says some fool. 'That's just a guitar from the olden days. I can play that.' Another chap says, 'Look, a symphony. That's just like a very big song! I bet I could write one of those.' And off they go.

The only good thing about pop stars going classical is that it's quite funny seeing them trying to look the part. Maybe it's the tuxedo (with basketball boots so people know they're still rock and roll). Maybe it's the constipated look as they try to conduct a 72-piece orchestra when they've only ever told a drummer what to do before. But mostly it's the bloody silly bow at the end. *Look at me! I'm classical! I must be, I'm bowing!*

PEOPLE WHO HAVE MEETINGS IN STARBUCKS
∾

O r Caffè Nero. Or Costa, or any one of a million identical coffee 'houses'. You see them, these sad would-be entrepreneurs, sitting around a too-tiny table crammed with laptops and empty sandwich wrappers, projecting flow charts for 08 and all this meaningless gobtoss. They're always so earnest about their meeting, largely because they realize one thing: that nothing says I AM A LOSER! more loudly and more clearly than having a business meeting in a café. Why not just have it at a bus stop? Or in your mum's front room? Nobody is ever going to believe that you have the ability to raise millions of dollars and run an international corporation if a) you haven't even got your own office, and b) you've got latte down your trousers.

TALKING HEADS
∾

T hose people on television who give their opinions, mostly on 'list shows'. There are three types of talking heads:

1. THE EXPERT KIND. Sometimes these are real experts in things like military history or stunt driving. Generally, they are experts in agreeing with the interviewer. Sometimes this is all too obvious, as when some 22-year-old nitlet professes a detailed knowledge of and love for the films of Buster Keaton, or when some TV presenter (see TV PRESENTERS) says he's read a book.

2. THE PROFESSIONAL TALKING HEAD. When they start off, they can be quite endearing, largely because they begin their 'careers' talking about things they might actually have some interest in, like pop music or

comedy. But as the years go by, they become corrupted by the lure of money and the chance to be almost recognized, sometimes. So they will appear in any show about anything. Heavy-metal photographers will try and look knowledgeable about lesbian cinema. Molecular scientists will suddenly find themselves having a favourite Benny Hill sketch. And, worst of all, political pundits will try and look as though they actually enjoy anything at all.

3. REAL FAMOUS PEOPLE. These can totally scupper a talking-heads type show. Because while it's brilliant that some researcher actually managed to get Steven Spielberg or Keith Richards or Lenin, the viewer can't concentrate on the interview for thinking, Why are they doing this? Are they secretly broke? Or are they just so vain that every time they see a TV camera they just have to talk to it?

PEOPLE WHO CALL THEMSELVES ECO-WARRIORS

～

Yes, actually call themselves that. While there's nothing wrong with saving the planet (there are surely very few things wrong about keeping the world going, although we could lose, say, the people who wrote *My Family* along the way and no harm done), the people who seem to have volunteered for the job are frequently tossbadgers.

Eco-warriors have all the virtues of the traditional British prat – smugness, self-satisfaction, lack of any sense of humour, being a bit too thin and healthy – combined with something new: the desire to Do Good but at the same time to Look Cool. That can't be right, surely. But no, off they go, driving into the jungle to save a lemur, hurtling across the sea in jet launches to protest about Japanese whale pies, dressing up as pretend soldiers to storm the walls of a factory. They're warriors! Eco-warriors! They have sexy sunglasses! They own accessories from camping shops! They work out! You want to punch and kick the whole sodding lot of them, you really do.

And why does everything they do have to be dramatic and eye-catching? Why is it all jeeps and powerboats and abseiling? It's just

James Bond (see JAMES BOND) for prats. And with all those boats and jeeps and exciting helicopter stunts, they must be buggering up the environment at a rate of knots.

PEOPLE WHO SAY,
'SO MUCH FOR GLOBAL WARMING'
∾

This can happen at any time. You're out walking the dog and it's a bit nippy out, or maybe you're in the pub's beer garden and it rained a bit earlier. And then suddenly, from nowhere, somebody walking past or sitting at the next table or (ideally) being dragged towards a waiting van by burly male nurses will look at you, shake their head, and say, 'Huh! So much for global warming!'

Yes. Because that's how it works. If we had global warming and it wasn't just an idea put about by communists, then instantly everywhere would be hot all the time and it would never rain or be a bit nippy ever again. That's science, that is. You knobstones.

VOLUNTARILY BALD MEN
∾

Going bald is rubbish. Having all your hair fall out makes you look like, at best, a former leader of the Tory Party or, at worst, a pervert from another planet. It's not alluring, it's not sexy, and as a reminder of fast-disappearing youth and time's winged chariot, it's only slightly less effective than sending yourself a telegram every day that reads ANOTHER DAY NEARER THE GRAVE!

So it seems slightly bizarre that for some sections of society – most notably builders, homosexuals and members of far-right organizations – baldness is a very cool and sexually attractive thing. A big shiny pate gleaming in the moonlight is apparently a massive turn-on. The look that blighted the middle years of Philip Larkin is cultivated by the chicer van driver. It's all very strange and makes about as much sense as trying to get women by knocking your own teeth out and replacing them with dentures.

PEOPLE WHO SAY,
'WOW! HAVE YOU BEEN TAKING ACID?'
❧

Well, it doesn't happen that often, but if somebody does say, 'Wow! Have you been taking acid?' in that special voice it means only this – 'Wow! I dislike either your idea or what you just said and in fact find it so alarming and shocking to my world view that the only way I can take it on board, or rather dismiss it, is by assuming that you were on drugs when you had/said it.'

In place of striking this hypothetical buffoon to the ground, why not remind them that most great ideas come from people who, at the time at least, were completely sober. That even in rock, where narcotics and ideas are often combined, the best and certainly the weirdest bits were invented before the drug pie was consumed. And that it is the crutch of a scoundrel to assume that just because Bozo Boy couldn't have an unusual idea if his brains were on fire, that you or anyone else needs a crack sandwich to come up with something different.

And then strike them.

PEOPLE WHO HATE AMERICANS
❧

All right, yes, fair enough, there are Americans who really do wear tartan golf hats and call themselves Hiram Hockenbocker III and say 'War Cess Tear Shear' when they mean Leeds and all that. And some Americans start wars and own hamburger companies and act in bad movies. So there is some cause for complaint, America-wise.

But this surely doesn't justify the kind of British twit who goes round saying that they hate Americans and they're all stupid and don't know where Africa is (it's underneath Corsica). Partly because a) who cares what you think, you're a maths teacher (see TEACHERS)? And b) this sort of person is in all other ways mad desperate keen to show how liberal and tolerant and not-racist they are. But if someone's wearing a tartan golf hat and holding a map of Luton upside down in the middle of Oxford Street, then it's okay to make wild generalizations and be a complete racist.

Of course, doing the same thing about Germans is unfair, but funny.

TEACHERS
∾

There are as many different kinds of teacher as there are people, which is no coincidence as many teachers are people. But for general purposes, teachers can be divided into the following groups:

1. LIBERAL TEACHERS. These are the teachers who started out with the best intentions – to change the world through education, to bring out the best in young people, and to instil values like fairness and equality in new generations. Time has not been kind to these

'Teachers were the caning, whacking, ear-twisting, Chinese-burning kings of school.'

teachers, and they spend breaktime behind the staff room smoking like murderers and taking large gulps from the school hipflask. Despite being on exactly the same wages as their colleagues, they somehow manage to look poorer than everyone else. Even the strange kid who lives in a skip with his grandparents and goes to school in a coal sack points at these teachers and says, 'Him be poor! I ate a bogie pie.'

2. STRICT TEACHERS. Once upon a time strict teachers ruled the world. They bestrode the plains of academe snorting great balls of flame from their hairy nostrils and giving detentions to everyone they met. They were even allowed to hit children, something that only other children are allowed to do nowadays. This seems astonishing now, but until the European Court of No Fun abolished corporal punishment, strict teachers were the caning, whacking, ear-twisting, Chinese-burning kings of school.

Now, however, they are, figuratively speaking, the castrati of education. Left weaponless in charge of a class full of future serial killers, their only weapon is sarcasm. Which is sadly only effective on the more sensitive and emotional pupils. All the other kids are immune to sarcasm, and will later burn down the teacher's house.

3. ARTS TEACHERS. These aren't really teachers, because no maths teacher ever said, 'Okay, kids, everyone just, like, do some maths until the bell goes, dig?' No French teacher ever invited the class to pretend to be an ant for half an hour. But this is what the people who teach drama and painting and sculpture and musical appreciation do. How can they stand the boredom? Because they've had some smack, that's how.

4. GAMES TEACHERS. Again, not really teachers. Not really people either. Just sort of machines for standing in fields shouting. And then, later, standing in changing rooms shouting. Sometimes, when all the children have gone home, games teachers can be seen running round the sports pitch, shouting at themselves.

5. HEAD TEACHERS. Once they were teachers, but now they're sort of managers, like the round bald man at Asda who spends all day telling off the checkout girls and staring wanly at the canned-goods section. Heads fill their lonely hours by standing at the window looking at the empty playground, going on conferences where they fail to cop off with other heads, and making long, incoherent speeches at assembly.

Heads like to pretend that they're modern, efficient figures who wear power suits and stride meaningfully down corridors both real and metaphorical. In fact, they secretly hanker for days of old, when they were called headmasters and headmistresses, and would stand in front of a Union Jack, dressed like Will Hay, and say things like, 'Some boy has been chewing in the fives court. If the culprit does not own up, the lower fifth will be hanged.'

PEOPLE WHO HATE DAN BROWN BOOKS

A n extraordinary writer, Dan Brown is notable for many things, not least of which is the fact that he has a name so boring, so dull and ordinary, that he might actually be a committee and his name might be an acronym. Did A Novel, Broke Records Of World Novelness. Something like that, anyway. But because of his huge success, notably the *Da Vinci Code* and lots of others called things like *The Retard Sanction* and *Atlantic Moss*, many people profess to hate Dan Brown.

True, he's not the world's greatest writer. True, he writes sentences like: 'Hell!' cursed Senator John Donkey as he slammed the phone slammily down. Fifty-six and silver-haired yet still with the youthful good looks that belied his many years working the oil rigs of the Persian Gulf, the senator cursed rudely and realized realizingly that he was – without question – trapped forever in a sentence from which he could never escape.'

But he is very popular and he writes what we used to call 'yarns'. Big, floppy adventure stories with cardboard people in them, that are escapist, ridiculous and page-turnerly. So why is he – and all the other lesser, not quite so wealthomatic, blockbuster people – so reviled? Is it because his books are easy to read, and easy things must also be bad things? Is it because he is successful and all successful people are bad evil murderers? Or is it because by hating Dan Brown and the rest, you are saying, 'Look! I didn't like the *Da Vinci Code*! And if I go on about it, people will think I must be really erudite and read only early twentieth-century Vorticist novels; when in fact I am an ill-informed snob who once got halfway through *Pride and Prejudice* and had to start again because I'd forgotten what it was about.' (See JANE AUSTEN.)

CELEBRITIES

If Andy Warhol had said, 'In the future everyone will be famous for bugger all', he'd have been even more right. We have long passed the point where people are even famous for being famous. That's long gone; now people are famous for wanting to be famous. They're famous for failing to become famous. Some are famous for knowing someone famous. It's revolting. What we thought was the Z-list turned out to be just the tip of the arseberg.

Jorge Luis Borges, who was famous for being excellent, wrote a story about a lottery that controlled every aspect of human life, where the wrong ticket could result in your execution and the right one could make you a king. Celebrity-wise, the world's not far from that now. Soon people won't actually have to do anything to become famous; they'll just be able to sit at home, waiting for the letter or email that says, 'Congratulations, Mister Thompson! You have been selected from millions of idle gimps to be famous! Tick here if you want as much publicity as humanly possible!'

CYCLISTS

They're still incredibly self-satisfied, smug, vain and humourless. Anyone who dresses like a condom on wheels has to be. Cyclists used to be wonderful features of British life, pedalling around in small family groups, smiling at the slothful pedestrians, looking forward to stopping at a country inn for a glass of dandelion and burdock and a lettuce salad sandwich. We were so fond of the bicycle that we made the police ride them, even though all the villains were driving large foreign cars or stealing trains.

But then a bad thing happened. The bicycle became a symbol not of eccentricity, but virtue. Owning a bicycle meant that you were an honorary eco-warrior (see PEOPLE WHO CALL THEMSELVES ECO-WARRIORS) and loved the Planet Earth, or 'Gaia' as you would call it after a couple of organic dandelion and burdocks. Riding to work at your overpriced wholefood store let you off all other duties, ecology-wise. You may be dressed like a corking tosser, but you were on a bike, and therefore almost Christ-like in your excellence (the phrase 'Christ on a bike' may derive from this idea, although it doesn't).

The worst thing is that bicycles are in fact secretly very bad for the environment. Their tyres are made of barely sustainable rubber, ripped from screaming plants in the Burmese jungle. Their frames are forged in huge furnaces, gears smelted in burning fires and factories in over-exploited developing countries, and the covering for the saddles is made of the hide of little baby mice. Probably.

RICKSHAW DRIVERS

༄

The very name 'rickshaw' is something of a misnomer, as it used to conjure images of determined Eastern pedalcab drivers, ringing their bells to scatter traffic as they conveyed their human cargo either to Raffles Hotel for a chota peg, or to the ancient temple to warn Sing Lu Sen of an attempt on her life.

The British rickshaw driver is not like that. He is usually a visitor to these shores too feckless to get bar work, who spends his days cycling about tinkling his bell at any woman he sees and then, when you have given in and agreed to go for a ride in his far-from-silver machine, reveals two things. One: he has never heard of where you want to go. And two: he will charge you twenty quid for the privilege of not getting there.

CYCLISTS 2

∾

Now that cyclists have the support of the environmental lobby and they've also got more and more of those little lanes with pictures of pushbikes on, cyclists are very full of themselves. It seems that owning a pair of silly shorts and a pointy helmet like the Green Goblin means that you are single-handedly preventing the heat death of the planet.

Unfortunately for the rest of us, it also means that you are gripped by an arrogance unheard of since the last days of the Hellfire Club. Cyclists now break every law known to man, except possibly playing football on a Sunday and not owning a falcon. They ride on pavements. They ride the wrong way down one-way streets. They fail to ring their tinkly dinkly bells when they are hurtling towards you. And they get violent when you challenge them. Which actually isn't that bad, because bikes nowadays are so easy to ride, with all those gears and so on, that cyclists are not as muscular as they used to be, and a puppy could have most of them.

OLD BLACK CAB DRIVERS

∾

That's not 'old drivers of black cabs'. There is nothing wrong with the elderly (although see OLD MEN IN GYMS). Wisdom and experience are good things, and should be harnessed. No, what is meant here is 'drivers of old black cabs'. For some reason, really old taxis – the smaller ones, with the snub nose, that you see in 1960s films – are quite possibly haunted. Or maybe it's just because they're old.

Whatever it is, you should never hail one. Ignore the fact that they're curiously keen to stop and pick you up. Never mind that shiny new cabs keep not stopping for you. Old black cabs – and their drivers – are a little bit too much on the Stephen King side of life.

You give in and hail one. It wheezes to a halt accompanied by what sounds like (and may even be) a saucepan full of old bolts. After several minutes of struggle in which firstly the driver can't hear you because he can't get his window down, and then you can't get the door open, you are off. The cab lurches forward as though the engine was about to be sick. You are thrown about the cab. The driver, who looks like the late Sir Anthony Blunt, tells you to mind the upholstery.

Your journey begins. The taxi takes no route you have ever seen. Perhaps it is relying on some mental map of the past, when it was happy and roamed the streets with its taxi friends. Perhaps it is the driver who thinks it is 1958. Either way, you are lost, late, and about to drive into the river.

Finally, after much swerving around corners and falling to the floor, you reach, if not your, then someone's destination. You step out, visibly rattled and quite possibly crippled. You offer the driver the fare. He is enraged because there's no tip.

After a mental debate, you do tip him, not because he is right, but because you don't want to wake up in the middle of the night and see a pair of headlights glaring at you malevolently from the foot of the bed.

CYCLISTS 3
∾

A nd then they have the nerve to shout, 'Get out of the road!' at you. *Okay – as soon as you get off the pavement, you self-satisfied, road-fearing, only-brave-because-you've-got-a-knobby-helmet-on, glorified-hobby-horse-riding tarmac wasters.*

OLD MEN IN GYMS
∾

G yms are full of machinery. Machines for running, machines for climbing, machines for – apparently – just ripping your arms right out of their sockets. These machines generally do their jobs quite well, if you actually use them properly (if you don't, you could end up wondering why your lungs are now wrapped around your head).

But some people have evolved their own uses for machinery. These people are called 'old men' and they use the whole gym in a different way to the rest of the world. They treat the machines more like a prop than a tool. They may look from a distance like they're 'working out', but in actual fact they are 'sitting on their arses', talking to their mates. Who are, of course, other old men. Sometimes the old men are having a kip on the machines. Sometimes they are lifting weights, in a cursory, occasional way. But mostly they are having a good old natter. Which is good in a way, as it means you can't go on the machines and you have to go and sit in the coffee bit until it's time to go home.

Where this all goes wrong, however, is when the old men decide to have their good old natter in the showers (see CHANGING ROOMS). Oh, lord.

YOUNG MEN IN GYMS

The illusion of superiority to one's fellow man is hard to keep up at the best of times, so imagine how much worse it is when you're at the gym. It's all very well pretending that you are a superb physical specimen when you have got all your clothes on and you're just walking past a home for the terminally obese (or Pizza Hut, as it's generally known).

But trying to maintain your fantasy of fitness in a gym is beyond most of us. There you are, gamely lifting something heavy and being almost sure that you felt a muscle in there somewhere. Suddenly a younger man comes in and starts virtually throwing weights into the air and catching them with his earlobes. At this point, you catch sight of yourself in the mirror. A large pile of old compost appears to have disguised itself as you.

PEOPLE WHO COMPLAIN

Complaining is, from time to time, a good and useful thing (see PEOPLE WHO DON'T COMPLAIN).

'That man is setting fire to our car!'

'Goodness! We should say something!'

But in all fairness, the preceding fictional example is about standing up for yourself, rather than complaining, which is defined by most dictionaries as: 'being a whingeing git who will try anything to ruin someone's day, so long as they can do it just by talking in a droney voice about someone else's perceived faults.'

Complaining is bad because it combines only negative elements. For a start, it offers no solutions. The old scumbollock who knocks on your front door because your ball has gone over his fence yet again rarely offers to buy you a PlayStation or suggest that you grow some leylandii (see LEYLANDII) so that your ball will bounce back into your own garden. No, he just wants to complain. Preferably while either handing you back a ball that has been deflated with some old-man scissors, or while hinting that somewhere, possibly in his shed or his odoury bedroom, there is a magical pile of balls, all collected over the years, some possibly signed by Bobby Moore, or even kicked over the wall by Bobby Moore as a lad.

Then there's the moany factor. If a stranger is just a friend you haven't met yet (and here's a clue: they aren't), then a complainer is just a lonely, stinky attention-seeker you haven't met yet. Complaining is the flip-side of making pals with people. Unable – thanks to their vile personalities, totally negative outlook, and obsession with keeping other people's footballs – to form normal relationships, complainers are forced to resort to a different tactic. Complaining.

When someone knocks on your door in the morning to complain about the fact that they could just about hear your Brian Eno CD after 10.30 p.m. if they stood on a ladder and jammed their ear up to the ceiling in a toothglass full of sophisticated surveillance equipment, they're not just there for the joy of making your life unpleasant. They're lonely and friendless and would do anything for human company.

Unfortunately, they are also very bad people who, when they die, will go to a special hell where demons will constantly kick footballs into their burning garden, play music loudly after ten thirty at night, take their milk from the fridge without replacing it, and never put the lid back on either the toothpaste or the toilet.

PEOPLE WHO DON'T COMPLAIN

~

This may well be a purely English phenomenon. Just as the English are a nation of whingekeepers (see PEOPLE WHO COMPLAIN), then they are also – by some strange paradox – a nation of apparent stoics in the face of a minor crisis. We can prove objectively that this problem is largely localized to England, incidentally, simply by looking at the rest of the world. In hot European countries, like France, Spain and Italy (there are others, but we need not name them all here), the populace are long used to rising up at any major grievance, such as the assassination of this week's president. In lesser ways, too, they are sensibly volatile. A minor parking infraction can lead to all sorts of honking of horns, waving of fists, and – if it's a particularly warm day – exchange of small-arms fire.

The same applies, of course, on other continents where it's a bit warm. From Indonesia to Argentina, when people get vexed, they take to the streets, do a lot of waving and shouting and, for some reason, set fire to all the buses. (NB: It's never really clear why buses come in for so much stick from the local populace. After all, very few buses have tried to suppress democracy. Then again, the bendy ones are almost certainly up to no good – see BENDY BUSES.)

And, of course, in the very cold countries, when people get vexed, they just drink vast amounts of rubbing alcohol, throw chairs at each other in bars made out of ice, and set fire to the buses. But that's probably more to keep warm than anything else.

So not complaining seems to be an activity confined entirely to the English (the rest of Great Britain, being Celts, have no truck with all that 'mustn't grumble' nonsense and even now are probably looking for some sort of bus to set fire to. The Cornish, not being real Celts, are thinking about torching an ice-cream van.) The English are famous throughout the world for not complaining. Here are some common phrases associated with not complaining and the English:

'MUSTN'T GRUMBLE.'

'WE DON'T WANT TO CAUSE A FUSS.'

'CAN'T COMPLAIN.'

'WE DIDN'T REALLY LIKE TO SAY ANYTHING.'

'THE CHICKEN WAS OFF BUT WE ATE IT ANYWAY.'

'I DON'T LIKE TO CAUSE A SCENE.'

'THE WAITER DID POUR THE SOUP OVER ALAN'S HEAD,
BUT WE DIDN'T TIP, SO THAT WAS ALL RIGHT.'

'I'M A COMPLETE CRAVEN COWARD SO PLEASE WALK ALL OVER ME.'

And so on. There is a fear seated deep in the English psyche that by causing a scene or making a fuss or saying anything other than 'thank you' to the person beating you up is somehow not the done thing. It's possibly a suspicion that maybe it's their fault all along, that somehow they made the nasty hotel receptionist give them a room with spiders in the minibar. And it's certainly something to do with the English belief that if you ignore something it will go away. Now, while this worked with, say, snoek, the Charleston and East 17, it never helps in a conflict situation. So the solution is clear: people who don't complain should – without becoming whiners – stand up for themselves and their rights. And then maybe the rest of the world will stop thinking of us as floppy-haired prannets in tweed socks.

PIRATES
∾

Very fashionable. One wonders, though, what other bunch of syphilitic mercenary psychopaths will become trendy next? Lawyers? Couriers? Opticians?

PEOPLE WHO LIKE BEING TAKEN SERIOUSLY
∾

One of the most overrated ambitions in the world, particularly in the entertainment industry – the desire to be taken seriously – has been responsible for the death of more fun than, say, hot-air ballooning or the last three *Star Wars* films. And yet it has spread through every area of modern life.

Obviously, sometimes this is not a bad thing. A brain surgeon who didn't want to be taken seriously is not somebody you'd like to have rooting around your cranium with a pair of pinking shears. Similarly, few of us would like to be in the same court as a judge who says, 'We find the defendant guilty of murder and sentence him to be hanged by the neck until – wait! I'm kidding! Fifty pounds' fine with costs! No! Hanging! No! I'm just messing with you! Yo! I'm also a rapper!'

But the world of entertainment exists for one purpose and one purpose only – to make people who have had a crappy day have a better one. People who are taken seriously – coal miners, shopkeepers, healthcare workers – like to go out, or come home, and not take things seriously. They don't care that the people entertaining them – clowns, jugglers, Morrissey – are perhaps in some ways silly or daft, they just want to be entertained.

This is not to say (not that it matters) that no entertainers can be serious. If your curse is that you are Ibsen, or Mahler, or Scott Walker, or any of the other great talents who can never remember a joke, let alone tell one, then fine. Be glum and be good at it. But everyone else! Shut up worrying about how important you are!

Sadly, this excellent advice is hardly ever – oh, the epic irony – taken seriously, and so the world of stuff that is meant to make us feel a bit less unhappy is instead frequently filled with gloom. Here is an easy, cut-out-and-weep guide to the major danger zones in the world of Being Taken Seriously:

1. ACTORS. Thirty years in the business, loads of experience, talent to spare (well, some of them) and finally, a nice part as the Reverend Bumblebee in *Midsomer Hernias*. Millions laughing, fairly genuinely,

at your hilarious portrayal of the foolish vicar. Maybe even a BAFTA. Possibly a shag. And what does your actor do? He gets fed up of being typecast as a jolly TV vicar, and jacks it in to go serious. Nobody ever wants to hire him again, he's not very good at it, and he ends his career playing Death in a room above a pub in Worthing (see also ACTORS).

2. AUTHORS. After their early hits with books like *The Reverend Bumblebee in Love* and *Bumblebee's Dilemma*, which sold by the crate-load and have found happy homes on shelves in bathrooms the world over, authors tend to get a bit gloomy around the onset of middle age (see CHARLES DICKENS). They lose the urge to tell stupid stories, and suddenly seek meaning. They get a bit too much into Martin Amis. And they write a five-million-word novel called *Over*, or *The Now Black*. Which does really badly but someone buys the film rights, changes it completely and calls it *More Bloody Cartoon Penguins*, and everyone's happy.

3. ROCK STARS. Every rock star ever has started out singing songs called 'Oo Yeah Woo Yeah' or 'Hey Mister Gnome I'm Over Here', songs that make up for in childishness what they lack in originality. And ten years later, where is your rock star? Off his noggin on wobble juice, standing on a stage dressed as Gardener's Question Time and singing something deep and meaningful about his life that's almost as long as his life.

4. COMEDIANS. Again, massive popularity due to one skill – making people laugh – puts them in a position to go off and do what they really want to do, namely play a tramp in a play. Or a 'Fool'. Or, oddly, a butler. Which is the sort of fact that would worry a butler.

5. TV PRESENTERS. The worst-case scenario of all. Because when you become a TV presenter, you are saying to the world, 'I know that I am a knobstone, but hey! I am smiley and will not do anything to annoy you.' But some of them break that contract with the audience, and go

and do something really silly like play a serial killer in a TV drama, or marry Bono.

MOBILE PHONE USERS
~

You can always tell if someone is a complete worthless arse by the way they use their mobile phones. If, for example, they talk without apparent interruption, it's not because they're having a chat with someone who's a good listener, it's because THEY DON'T KNOW WHEN TO SHUT UP. The reason it sounds as though there's nobody on the other end is not because they're so lonely that they have to pretend they're talking to someone (although that might easily be the case), it's because they are so sub-crustaceanly rude that not only do they not know the difference between a conversation and a monologue, they don't care.

This also explains why these worthless nobulons only seem to know one pronoun: 'I'. 'I did this' and 'I said that' for hours and hours. In a sane, polite society, surely we could invent a phone that delivers a small electric shock (or even a big, brain-melting one, it's all the same thing) to anybody who uses the word 'I' more than a thousand times in one minute? It doesn't seem unreasonable (see PEOPLE WITH HUGE EGOS).

PEOPLE WITH HUGE EGOS
~

Surely there was a time when having an ego was a bad thing? By 'ego', this book doesn't mean 'a sense of self-awareness', that's quite a useful thing, especially if you haven't got any trousers on and you're making your maiden speech to the House of Lords. No, the word 'ego' here means 'massive and utterly unfounded belief that everything you say or do is incredibly interesting just because you are the person saying or doing it'.

You can't open a newspaper these days without (see YOU CAN'T OPEN A NEWSPAPER THESE DAYS WITHOUT …) seeing some piece of print onanism where somebody whose views change with the temperature of their earwax is going on about something that a) they know nothing about, b) they care nothing about, and c) they probably wrote a column about last month which stated a completely opposite point of view. This wouldn't be so bad, but they always have to drag everything back to themselves. 'This new law will cause hardship for millions. I know, because I saw a tramp once.' GO TO HELL!

And that's before we get into the world of the fawning interview and its cousin, the celebrity autobiography. There is something about the sight – or maybe it's the smell, a faint odour of musk and diamonds – of celebrities that makes intelligent people and journalists go all wobbly at the brain. Yes, they are prettier than us, and richer, and have our entire lifetime sex ration in one evening, but the only thing they have in common with everyone else is that when they open their mouths they're no more or less interesting than the rest of us. And as they spend all their waking hours on telly, talking about themselves, chances are high that they ran out of interesting stuff to say a long, long, long time ago.

PEOPLE WHO USED TO BE FAMOUS
∾

Yes, we know. People come up to you all the time and say, 'Didn't you used to be X?' Well, serves you right for being famous then. And for telling everybody when you were famous that, oh, you'd give anything to not be famous again.

PEOPLE WHO WERE NEARLY FAMOUS
∾

Sometimes you feel sorry for them – that one wrong decision which crossed the thin line between eternal fame and working in a chip shop – then you look at their faces. Their strange, not-rich, not-poor faces, which can't make up their minds if they're the faces of people who were nearly famous and long to be sitting on the lap of fame, or people who don't care about being famous and are just Normal. Although not with that fake tan, gold chain and 'hairstyle' you're not.

PEOPLE WHO WENT TO SCHOOL
WITH SOMEONE FAMOUS
◦

Don't go to their gigs when they come to your town. Don't show the reporter from your local paper all your school photos. Don't go on *This Is Your Life* and weakly shake their hand as they try to remember who you are. Buy a high-powered rifle and shoot them. They're famous and you're not! What's wrong with you! (NB: If you do shoot anyone famous, don't say you got the idea from this book. That would just make YOU look silly. Probably best to not shoot anyone at all.)

TV PRESENTERS
◦

They don't seem to know anything. Time was when a TV presenter was at worst a jobbing actor with a nice voice (see ACTORS) and at best a polymathic journalist and historian who'd sailed the Amazon in a kayak to interview Fidel Castro. But these days … It looks like the TV companies just send a van round the hair salons of the land with the words FREE CONDITIONER INSIDE THIS VAN! GET IN THE VAN! IT'S PERFECTLY SAFE!

You can understand it with the kids' TV presenters. There's not much need for intellectual rigour or a deep-veined knowledge of the Middle East when all you have to do is talk to a toy animal and introduce some other toy animals. It's not even completely mind-offending with the teen and youthy presenters. Never mind the fact that they've only learned to read autocues and keep staring at books, wondering when the page is going to move down; never mind the fact that they can only communicate by waving their arms and shuffling about on their backsides, like a man who's been glued to a toilet trying to get help. All they have to do is interview soap stars and pop stars, who are equally ill-prepared for taking GCSEs, buying things with coins or any other rigorous tests of the mind.

All that's fine. What is a little bit vexing is the fact that newsreaders and current-affairs presenters seem to be going the same way. No wonder the world is in a terrible state. Thirty years ago, a good TV interviewer could reduce a president or a prime minister to tears just by ripping apart their domestic transport policy. Now an incisive interview with a politician doesn't go much further than a pretty lady disguised as a real news reporter saying to a major political figure, 'I like your shoes. Where did you get them?'

TV PRESENTERS 2
∾

And what happened to talking proper? All right, so a full-on return to the bollock-throttling vocal styles of the 1950s isn't necessarily a good thing. But it would be nice to have presenters who had some vague grasp of normal patterns of speech. It's not as if they all come from tiny villages deep in the heart of the Auvergne. Most of them are putting on a completely made-up glottal Estuary media Cockernortherny accent anyway.

It's all good for sales of the *Radio Times* anyway, since if you can't understand what the stone-chewing inarticulatists are saying, you can just go and look it up in a listing mag, and pray it doesn't say, '7.30 – Cawnashem Speet'.

SCIENTISTS
∾

Science used to be our friend. It eradicated disease! It made labour-saving devices! It shortened distances and aided communication! It was like Superman, only instead of one man in a dim costume, it was loads of men and women in white coats, all working round the clock to try and make things less crap.

And it worked for ages. Things did become a lot less crap. Despite the claims of several religious groups, life is a lot better now that a) we don't have to pretend that we're all going to one of two made-up places, b) we can have it off with any grown-ups we feel like, and c) everyone knows that any bloke in a robe who claims to represent the creator is at best misguided and at worst a kiddy fiddler. So hurray for science and reason.

But now it seems to have got a bit odd. Those lovely scientists are cloning each other and growing giant cabbages and generally doing the big science equivalent of taking the back off the watch and pulling all the bits out without really knowing how to get them all back in again. They tell us they are doing so in the pursuit of knowledge. A special knowledge that comes on rectangular pieces of paper with numbers and pictures of presidents and queens on it (no, not stamps).

PEOPLE WHO YOU'VE NEVER HEARD OF WRITING THEIR MEMOIRS
～

Who are you? Why have you written a book? Is the title of your book your catchphrase? Why are you smiling on the cover? Are you a pop singer? A page-three model? A former leader of the Conservative Party? What's going on?

PEOPLE WHO ARE FAMOUS FOR ONE THING AND THEN GO AND DO ANOTHER THING
～

You know. Like gardening experts who write novels. Or actresses who 'invent' perfumes. Or rock stars who exhibit their horrible paintings. People like that. There should be a special Celebrity Law which covers the activities and maintenance of famous people, and one of the first stipulations of this excellent new Celebrity Law should be that EVERYONE WHO IS FAMOUS CAN BE FAMOUS FOR ONE THING AND ONE THING ONLY. Otherwise it's just annoying.

PEOPLE WHO ARE REALLY, REALLY, REALLY FAT
～

Once – as we are always being told in the sort of columns that tell you things you could have worked out for yourself if you weren't so busy reading columns – it was a sign of wealth and importance to be fat. (Even though most paintings and statues and so on of interesting historical figures – Jesus, Shakespeare, Beethoven, Napoleon,

Florence Nightingale – show them to be of slender to average build. And also even though most of history's gits – George III, Mussolini, Nero, Michael Moore – have clearly dined often and on lard.) Whatever the truth of that theory, these days it is clear that rich people are thin and poor people are fat. The difference is so marked that banks no longer ask your income when you apply for an account, they just weigh you.

It's completely wrong. Setting aside the horrible irony that the very poor of the world are starving while the moderately poor could live off their own body fat for years at a time, it suggests that not only do the superwealthy have all the dosh, they also have all the healthy food. While the lowerly waged spend their lives sticking 'pizzas' (i.e. flat loaves of bread covered in dinner snot) and burgers (claws and beaks and fins) and fizzy drinks (carbon dioxide in a diluted sugar sauce) into their surely weeping digestive systems, rich people are living on nice green food and fresh fruit.

The life of a peasant was famously, again in one of those columns, said to be 'nasty, brutish and short'. These days, the life of a poor person in the West is what? Boring, brutish and obese? Ears and eyes filled with bad telly and guts filled with bad food?

Perhaps it's deliberate. By adding mass to the masses, they can't rise up and overthrow the ruling classes because they can't get off the sofa. Feed people enough chemicals and E numbers and they'll settle into a state of such comatose apathy that only the sight of a *Big Brother* contestant actually exploding on television will wake them up (see REALITY TELEVISION). Or maybe the aliens who really rule the world are just fattening us up.

TELEVISION, MUSIC
& FILM

EUROVISION
~

Oh God oh God oh God oh God.

BBC VERSUS ITV
~

They were so different once. One was austere and grey and talked nicely and wanted us to better ourselves, but not too much in case we liked it and took over. The other was funny and vulgar and liked America and made a lot of noise and wanted us to win money and prizes and go mental. It was rather nice, like having two different aunts, one of whom always gave you a really dull book for Christmas but always looked after you, while the other gave you £20 and a PlayStation but was too pissed to make Christmas dinner. Between the two of them, they pretty much had things sorted out.

But now the differences between them seem to have blurred. The BBC has decided to become zippy and modern and have bad soaps (see AFTERNOON SOAPS and, worse, reality shows (see REALITY TELEVISION), and generally try to look like an ageing librarian out on the town with his nephews. Meanwhile, ITV have started making crappy crime dramas and Jane Austen adaptations (see JANE AUSTEN). These days the only way to tell them apart is that ITV game shows use a lot of blue lighting and BBC ones favour liberal use of red. Bit like party conferences, really.

EUROVISION 2
~

The thing is with the Eurovision contest … it's where do we begin to tell the story of how crap a thing can be? For a start, what is

'Eurovision'? Has anybody ever seen one? Is it a company? A technique? A pseudonym for one of the Transformers? Nobody seems to know, but it's been around since the 1950s, so it's probably a war crime. Only joking.

Secondly, whose idea was the Song Contest? Because if there's one thing we can be absolutely sure about regarding the countries of Europe, it's that you don't want to be stirring up national rivalries with that lot. These are countries who've gone to war over the most trivial matters – the shooting of an Archduke; the question of who's got the real Pope – so having a contest based on something really important like music is bordering on madness.

In fact, the main criterion for joining would appear to be that your nation has recently been involved in a bloody conflict. So when the Contest started, it was all the people who'd been in the last big war.

'Oh God oh God oh God oh God.'

Then in the 1960s and 70s new sites of violence like Israel and Cyprus got involved. And after that? Serbia, Bosnia, places like that. One can only surmise that Estonia got in by lying to the selection panel and claiming to have had a war that nobody saw happen.

EUROVISION 3

And the big 'joke' of Eurovision – the thing that made us Brits watch even when it was really, really awful? It was the idea that everyone else was rubbish, and even though our entries (Cliff) were also rubbish, they were less rubbish than the foreigners' stuff, and so we could simultaneously put forward rotten songs and sneer at other people for doing the same.

Because we kept winning. Fairly often. (All right, we didn't beat Abba, but we surely knew how to rip them off – Brotherhood of Man, Bucks Fizz, and so on.) And as long as we were winning, that was all right. Britain is, after all, the greatest pop-and-roll nation in the world, apart from America, who aren't allowed to enter the Eurovision Song Contest.

So we were also allowed to find everything hilarious because we were the best and everyone else was crap. But then something happened. Two things happened, in fact. First of all, the Europeans started getting better. They entered people who could write songs. They had catchy Eurodisco tunes. And they discovered wit (remember that Finnish death-metal band? Noël Coward couldn't have done it better.)

The other thing that happened – the really awful yet totally predictable thing – was that we went rubbish. We started entering acts that were even worse than, say, *Doctor Who* in the 1980s. We completely lost the plot. By 2007 you could have entered some human hair in a box and it would have been better than the official British entry.

The solution seems obvious. We must either find someone who can write some decent songs – not easy, in this country – or withdraw gracefully, citing a musical headache of national proportions. Because soon, very soon, Terry Wogan will have nothing to take the piss out of. And that's got to be wrong.

TV TALENT SHOWS
∾

Note the use of the word 'talent'. These shows exist as much to display lack of talent as they do ability. And the sight of the 'judges' – dull, scripted people who are only there to scrape a bit of money out of the soon-to-be discarded husks of the performers – telling the hopefuls that they are no good is appalling. The judges' sole qualification for the job is vanity and the ability to talk in clichés that someone else has written for them. Artificial, stiff, egotistical and dull, they make the manufactured groups they represent look organic and thrilling.

TV TALENT SHOWS 2
∾

Worst of all, this kind of drosswallop is a throwback to the days before fun. Talent shows may well go back hundreds of years, but so what? So does smallpox. It's as though, as the music industry dies (see DEATH OF THE MUSIC INDUSTRY), it acts like that computer in 2001 and reverts to its long-distant youth, dropping all claims to hipness and just being some last naff, desperate Tin Pan Alley attempt to hoick a few groats off the hoi polloi.

'Talent shows may well go back hundreds of years, but so what? So does smallpox.'

CHAT SHOWS – THEN
∾

The Americans seem to have started them. They were always the same. After some gabbling from an invisible man, a bloke in a 70s suit (well, it was the 1970s, fair enough) would come on to the set to the kind of applause that surely only the Second Coming would merit, tell some 'jokes' that were really just newspaper headlines rejigged, and then talk to the band leader, who was sycophantic in a way that would have worried Uriah Heep. Then he would interview three famous people, one at a time. ('Interview' in this context does not mean grill, debrief or even extract useful information from. It means 'praise excessively and encourage to promote their latest project'.) Sometimes there would be a band. Always there would be a commercial break.

In Britain – and presumably other countries – this model was not taken up, because in them days all chat shows were on the BBC and the BBC was not the kind of place where you came on and told jokes (see THE BBC VERSUS ITV). The British chat show was therefore a reverential affair, with frequent apologies for being too personal and lots of pauses for the host to laugh his face off at some God-awful showbiz anecdote.

It was horrible, but what replaced it, amazingly, was worse.

CHAT SHOWS – NOW
❦

They're not what they were, you know. Mind you, what they were was pretty bad, so in a sense chat shows have gone from bad to still bad. What happened was that in America chat shows were evolving in the sense that they were getting smarter. Possibly fed up with the solid wall of gammy gloss and sponsorship horror, the newer chat shows were more cynical, looser and more inclined to send up their guests. This was a good thing, for a while. Unfortunately, they're still doing it, and some of the hosts have been doing it for so long – sending up guests, mocking the format, and so forth – that the viewer just wonders why they're still doing it if they hate it that much, and changes channels.

In Britain, as ever, the format was adapted. The new chat shows here had the same mixture of irony and mockery but, with few exceptions, what they also had was a lethal combination of rubbish hosts and worse guests. So instead of the biggest stars in Hollywood being ribbed by the best stand-ups in the world, here you had a 'star' you'd never heard of – being mildly insulted by the bloke who'd come fourth in the Perrier Awards three years ago. It wasn't the same.

And yet, instead of shooting the format and hurriedly kicking it under the carpet, TV bosses stuck with it, believing (wrongly) that they could put any old TV presenter (see TV PRESENTERS) or useless comic or radio DJ into the host's chair and it would be fine. It's not fine. It's never fine.

ANTIQUES SHOWS

They used to be sort of forums where middle-class people would go and be reassured. Now they are used, brilliantly and wrongly, as afternoon fillers. Beefy couples in ill-fitting sweatsuits are forced to go to markets in the rain to look at bits of old lamps and one-eyed

'The whole thing is not only deeply depressing but also encourages people to buy as much old toot as possible.'

stuffed rats. Worse, they are made to hang around with bowtie-faced professional patronizers who apparently make a living running antique shops. The whole thing is not only deeply depressing but also encourages people to buy as much old toot as possible in the vain, dead hope that one day it will be worth a spillion quid. Such things can destroy the morale of a nation.

GADGET SHOWS

Wow. Here's a man who'd like to be younger than he is. Here's a woman who'd like to be working on another show and any show will do so long as the man who'd like to be younger than he is won't be on it. Here's a set so cheap you can see through it. And here's the pitch! They review brand-new gadgets. Wow again. By 'reviewing' they mean 'talking about' and 'pressing the buttons on', and by 'brand-new gadgets' they mean 'any old rubbish a pretend Japanese company has got lying around the office'. And this is the future.

BREAKFAST TELEVISION

Who thought it would be a good idea to have television before toast? In American movies we sometimes see people having a coffee and a waffle while watching glamorous presenters interviewing Hollywood stars before 9 a.m. In Britain we have slightly mad-looking people who don't seem to have had enough sleep interviewing, well, each other. This isn't too bad – it is, after all, one of the central planks of entertainment – but before you've had your boiled egg? It seems excessive.

POP TELLY

It's over. All the great shows that glided on the ocean of telly when the world was young have been cancelled. The basic idea of getting the groups in to mime and smile to their hits – a fantastic, art-school concept that if it had been thought of by a Slade (the art school, not the group) graduate would be winning prizes everywhere – has been superseded by not one but three rotten things.

1. The idea that television has to be real. So instead of having top bands pretend to perform what is, after all, the ideal version of their song – i.e. the one they spent eight squillion dollars and three years recording – they get them to perform it live. That is, out of tune and out of breath with rotten sound through cheap TV speakers.

2. The idea that just seeing people sing a song is not enough. So instead of seeing some people sing a song, we get some bad director's rehash of either a film he saw when he was high on skunk, or some dancing women in their underwear smiling as the pop star walks out pretending to mumble.

3. Similar to point 1, but even more horrid, the televised live concert. Not only does this have the demerit of being out of tune, and so forth, but also it means that a) you get an audience singing along and waving their mobile phones at the camera (see MOBILE PHONES) and b) instead of seeing the band do their hit and shove off, you have to sit through all their other songs as well, which is no fun whatsoever. And – just to add injurious insult to insulting injury – they project their new video behind themselves so as to remind the younger set what they are enduring.

REALITY TELEVISION
⌀

The bastard who came up with the title *Big Brother* for a reality show may be more cynical than previously advertised. Because if there's one thing that perfectly sums up your *1984*-style Orwellian prolefeed culture, it's the replacement of actual real content with made-up stuff. Newspapers and news-media stuff were originally designed to transmit information about events that had happened largely uncontrollably – wars, famines, earthquakes. Now they just tell us the adventures of someone who passed an audition. And by audition, they don't

'And by audition, they don't mean a display of performing skill.'

mean a display of performing skill, they mean 'were prepared to show off their personality disorder in public'.

In *1984*, the news channels showed footage from possibly made-up wars, interchangeable names of adversaries, and randomly selected hate figures. These days *I'm a Celebrity Get Me Out of Here* is our Oceania, the *Big Brother* house is Airstrip One, and *Heat* magazine is alternately the Ministry of Love and Hate Week.

REALITY TELEVISION 2
∼

And it's not real. Reality TV is the news – i.e. real things happening to real people in real places. Unless life is all staged for the benefit of some higher power and the world's a stage and so forth, there isn't anyone with a script going, 'And cue the economic collapse of Mali!' or similar. Whereas Reality TV is, if not completely staged (and any television worker will tell you, if plied with strong drugs, that every show is as manipulated and directed as possible), then as carefully planned as possible, from the cast (contestants) to the storyline (introducing new people and challenges).

Eventually, and it already seems to be happening, reality shows will become as ritualistic and formalized as your Japanese Noh play, and every contestant will know their place and every narrative will unfold according to a series of unwritten rules, and the name 'Reality TV' will just be a phrase like 'mystery plays' or 'Morris dancing', whose original meaning has changed completely over the years.

They'll still be crap, though.

THE DEATH OF THE SITCOM
∽

A few months ago, the death of the sitcom was all the rage. Apparently, both as a commercial venture and as an art form, the situation comedy is no longer valid. Fifty years of good, bad, great and bloody awful television has come to an end.

Except, of course, it hasn't. They're still making them. In America, they're enormously successful. In Britain, we still make some incredibly good ones. So why are people saying it's dead? Because they're TV executives and they'd like to stop making sitcoms because sitcoms aren't as cheap as reality shows (see REALITY TELEVISION). And anytime somebody doesn't want to do something, they say it's dead.

Try this at home, kids! When your mum tells you to go to bed, and you don't want to go to bed, tell her you can't because 'the bed is dead'. See? Now you're a TV executive!

DOCUMENTARIES
∽

Leaving aside the whole business of documentaries being essentially light-entertainment packages when once they could bring down governments (well, weedy governments), they also seem to have stopped being about what they're supposed to be about. This is because they're presenter-led. So if you turn on the telly one night hoping to watch something about nuclear weapons or a famous painter or a funny country, good luck. Because what you will get is a programme that's more about the presenter/host/documentary-maker than the alleged subject. He or she will manage to get in every frame, to interrupt every interviewee, and, in case you foolishly close your eyes, to add on a voiceover that contains the word 'I' more times than an egomaniac's phrasebook.

EASTENDERS
~

I t might seem an easy target but what the hell? *EastEnders* might just be the single most annoying thing in the world. It can, on a good day, stun a sugar-crazed toddler into frightened silence. And on a bad day it can make you take off your shoe and smash your telly into tiny glass and plastic buttons.

Why is it so bad? It's only a soap, after all. Perhaps it's because it's sold as being entertainment when in fact it exists in a parallel universe to entertainment. If the producers of *EastEnders* had been honest from the start and said, 'We've invented a show which is specifically designed to depress people and to make them want to die,' then that would have been all right. *EastEnders* might even have won awards for being innovative and daring in its open hatred of the human race and its totally bleak, Alban Berg-like view of the sheer pointlessness of existence. But instead they claim that it's meant to be somehow pleasurable to watch. That the dead-eyed semi-actors who walk through the grey streets of Walford and exchange empty words and meaningless actions are apparently great fun to be with. That the astonishing contrast between the utterly, utterly boring, unconvincing dialogue and the insane, childish, cartoon action is possibly something a non-sociopath might get pleasure from.

The only interesting thing about *EastEnders* is that it has succeeded in doing what the Luftwaffe failed to do: to destroy the East End of London. Consider this – before *EastEnders*, the popular view of most people concerning the East End was that it was full of cheerful, jolly, roguish Cockneys who might be a bit annoying – the Scousers of London – but who were essentially good, witty people whose rough exteriors concealed hearts of gold. Now, thanks to *EastEnders*, everyone thinks that being born within the sound of Bow Bells means you are a mean-spirited, humourless, sour-faced, tight-lipped, grey-skinned, screaming, mumbling idiot. Well done, *EastEnders*! Well done!

CORONATION STREET
∾

The first great British soap opera – over forty years old – and contemporary with a wave of northern social realism. Shows like *Coronation Street* and *Z Cars* were slightly less gritty, but still strong, cousins to films like *Saturday Night, Sunday Morning* and *The Loneliness of the Long Distance Runner.* Yes, they were.

And if it seems astonishing to make that claim now, well, blame the near half-century process of not so much dumbing down as dulling down *Coronation Street.* It was a unique show in its day, and now it isn't. In the 1960s, 70s and even the 80s, the Street was an extraordinary mixture of things: down-to-earth Lancashire realism, mild social comment, soapy excitement, and wit. *Coronation Street* was funny; rooted in both a world of tough northern women and slightly camp northern men, it brought humour and genuinely smart comedy to a genre that's always been famous for being utterly humourless (see *EASTENDERS*).

Nowadays, perhaps because it's written by people who've 'always wanted to write for *Coronation Street*' because they've been watching it for years – but must have been pissed when they watched it, because they seem to have no idea of what the show was all about – *Coronation Street* is now a stupid mixture of weak plots and worse action. Its best features look anachronistic. Its worst features are probably the future of British soap.

AFTERNOON SOAPS
∾

Not Australian ones (see AUSTRALIAN SOAPS), which at least have the virtue of both sunny weather and attractive cast members, but home-made British soaps. These are really scary. They are, for obvious reasons, always shot in foul weather, and always have to feature at least four doctors. The cast are a procession of people either on their way up and so in the show for just two months, or those on the way down who wince when you remember that they once starred in *Blake's 7* or *The Onedin Line*. And, worst of all, people who have always been in afternoon soaps and have never seen themselves on the telly after four o'clock.

AUSTRALIAN SOAPS

Nobody really knows why or how the craze for Australian soap operas took hold in this country; possibly the nice weather or the nice-looking people or just the overall niceness made them so

'Australians used shows like Neighbours *and* Home and Away *to escape their homeland and invade ours.'*

popular, a window into a sort of 1950s world where it was always sunny and everyone acted like a Girl Guide on her day off.

But Australian soaps were really an entertainment-world Trojan horse. Australians used shows like *Neighbours* and *Home and Away* to escape their homeland and invade ours. They became pop stars, and actors, and models, and some of them even made it into the movies. And now, having accomplished their mission like a specially designed virus, the Australian soap is returning to its native land, its work completed. Until next time …

AMERICAN SOAPS
∾

We don't really seem to like them that much. If you discount the Big Two Ds from the 80s – *Dallas* and *Dynasty* – which were so huge and glossy and studded with diamonds that they crushed every squeak of opposition under their mighty heels forever – then most American soaps have never really done that well in the UK.

And it's not because our tastes are too parochial. We watch all kinds of American nonsense, and the good stuff too. It is, jaw-droppingly, because American soap operas are WORSE THAN OURS. Let's just think about this for a second. The average, standard American soap opera is worse than *Coronation Street*. It's worse than *Emmerdale*. It's even worse than *EastEnders*. It might even be – can this be possible? – worse than *Hollyoaks*.

Stunning, isn't it? But close inspection reveals this to be the case. American soaps, which are primarily 'daytime' because at night they're out hunting for victims and drinking their blood, are all called things like *As the World Gets Worse* or *The Days of Our Crappy Lives*. They all star really good-looking people who look stupid because a) they all work in banks or shops and they look like gods, and b) they are dressed like Norwegian pimps, all blond and tanned and jewel-infested. The acting is – again, unbelievably – worse than that in British soaps. People stare at their co-performers as though the lines they can't remember are written on their foreheads. People recite their dialogue like it was a phone number. And the plots always seem to involve either an alien abduction that turned out to be a dream – or a dream that turned out to be an alien abduction.

FILMS AND TV PROGRAMMES THAT WERE MADE IN BLACK AND WHITE

They don't like showing them on the telly, you know, because they look old-fashioned. Of course they look old-fashioned, you telly prat, because they're old. That's the idea. They might also be brilliant, or hilarious, or inventive, or shocking. They might be *Laurel and Hardy*, or *Un Chien Andalou*, or *Casablanca*, or an old *Doctor Who*, or the *Steve Allen Show*. But they're old and in the way, and not in colour, so why bother?

'Of course they look old-fashioned, you telly prat, because they're old. That's the idea.'

Of course, this doesn't apply to anything modern made in black and white to look cool and arty, like a rock video, or a short film. They're in black and white, true, but they're new. So they're not old. It all makes sense.

ACTORS
∾

Paid weirdos. Acting is one of the strangest professions in the world. For a start, unlike being a doctor, a lawyer or a prostitute, it's not really a profession, in the sense that professions are things where you learn a useful skill that's hard. Actors are essentially paid to dress up as other people and go round saying things that other people wrote. And they call it work.

The most annoying thing about actors – and there be plenty – is that they really do take it all incredibly seriously. They call it 'the Craft', as though they also managed to fit in a bit of basket-weaving and macramé in between going to rehearsals and wearing cravats a lot. They suffer for their art. They have breakdowns. They dig deep into their souls and come up with the goods. It all makes you want to punch them through a hedge.

Actors are like this, not because the whole process of mining one's very heart and soul is difficult. They are like it because a) they are all barmy, and b) most of them are out of work nine months of the year, which makes them a little bit … insecure – to say the least. To say the most, it makes them absolutely neurotic barmy mental cases.

ACTORS 2
∾

Not only that, they seem duty bound to have opinions about stuff. Now, everyone is – you may have heard this idea before – entitled to their own opinions. Most of us are even entitled to other people's opinions. But every opinion does not carry the same weight. The opinion of, say, Nelson Mandela on a variety of topics – jail, racism, colourful shirts – may be said to have a certain heft because not only is he a very intelligent man but he has also had experience of all these things.

An actor, however, has not. This is not because they have never experienced jail, racism and so on. They have, but in a play. Or a film. Or an advert. Actors – for whom reality is always less appealing than fantasy, because fantasy is a world of adventure and applause, whereas reality is a bedsit in Clapton – cannot tell the difference between acting and real life.

And so it is quite probable that when some twit off the stage is on telly, banging on about injustice and badness, or taking part in a sketch on a charity show with some people who did do the research, that he or she might actually think that they spent six months in a Congolese jail.

STAGE ACTING
∾

The worst kind of acting. Maybe about forty hundred years ago this sort of thing made sense. The stage drama is like its cousin, the opera. Opera has nothing to do with real singing and acting, unless you think of it as being the *Lord of the Rings* re-enacted by Meat Loaf. So, too, stage acting has nothing to do with real acting and drama and so forth.

There's a trend towards realism in drama these days, which can be dull – IT'S A STORY FOR GOODNESS' SAKE! – but even so, they have a point. Suspension of disbelief works best when someone's made the effort. And it's a sad fact that even the worst soap opera (see EASTENDERS) look and sound more real than the best stage play.

For a start, there's the shouting. Even with hidden mikes and so forth, actors instinctively sense that they are on a stage with a lot of people staring at them from several yards away. So they bellow their lines.

'Come in, Mister Hatherley! And be quiet! Mother is ASLEEP!'

And so on. God help anyone with sensitive ears if there's an Ibsen-type moment of despair.

'Your uncle … is dead, Mrs Stocknorken.' Followed by that keening noise of anguish that only actors do, which is the stage equivalent of the slowed down 'NOOOOOOOOOOOOOO!!!', only a lot funnier.

'Maybe about forty hundred years ago this sort of thing made sense.'

And it's not just the shouting. There's the make-up, and the sets, and the sound effects. The whole thing looks like a sort of self-parody, as if the actors have suddenly noticed that the play is rubbish and the only way out is to send it up. Even modern, trendy plays, with video screens and computer graphics and so forth, are just covering up the cracks, in the way that a West End musical will have a spectacular set so nobody notices that the songs are all duff.

FILM ACTING

Not like other acting. For a start, a lot of the time they don't have any rehearsals. This makes stage actors feel special, and makes film actors sad, because they don't get to do an actor's all-time favourite arsey thing – go to a rehearsal. Rehearsals give actors the chance to play 'Woman Going to a Rehearsal' or 'Man Reading *The Times* in BiFocals'.

Film actors just have to get on with it. But at least they also don't have to learn the whole flaming script. Just the two pages they'll be filming today if they're not too off their chumps on specially made hand-tooled glitter cocaine beforehand. And they can do it again if they get it wrong. And again. And again.

In fact, when you think about it, film acting is totally easy. They even encourage you not to 'act'. The camera picks up your slightest gesture or eye movement, you see. And so it's probably best if you don't move at all, or raise your voice, or do anything. Just stand in front of the camera like it was an old Victorian portrait camera, freeze, and say the line in a sort of reluctant way. Then go back to your enormous trailer, read your emails and have a kip. Three weeks later a cheque for eighteen squillion pounds will arrive and you can go and buy some more glitter cocaine.

'BACKSTORY'

One of the many things that are very, very annoying about actors (see ACTORS) is that they can't just do their jobs. They have to ask a lot of stupid questions. In this, they are like children, except kids are capable of learning (and, unlike actors, eventually they grow up). But actors keep going, *Why? Why? What's my motivation? Why does my character say this? Why haven't I got more lines? Why isn't the film named after me?* And, worst of all, *What's my character's backstory?* If you've never come across the concept of backstory before, well, bully for you. It is a big old compost-heap of an idea, and causes much aggravation where once there was peace. The idea of 'backstory' is that the Character – Mr Jobbly, The Killinator, Skinny Doris or whoever – has had an existence before the film or play started. They weren't just made up by someone, you know! They have lives.

Of course they were just made up by someone. They don't have lives. They have no existence at all. But the actor finds this unsatisfying. It's not something that's going to lead to any more dialogue, is it? There's no work in not existing. So they decide that they will give the character a backstory. A life before the film.

Sounds harmless? It isn't. Five minutes into the first scene, where all Mr Jobbly has to do is buy a magazine and agree to meet his cousin in a bar, the actor is naked and crying on the floor. Why? Because in the backstory Mr Jobbly never learned to read and the purchase of a magazine is just a cover for his deep and real sadness.

It's a shame robots can't act, it really is (see ROBOTS).

SCIENCE-FICTION ACTING
∽

It's different to proper acting. For some reason, playing an alien or a robot and so on seems to give actors a new lease of annoyingness. Maybe it's the knowledge that as nobody, certainly not the writer, knows what aliens and robots say and do, the actor – for once in his life – knows just as much as anyone else about the subject.

Despite this, they still manage to bring their own unique brand of actorish trickery and nonsense to the role. Here are just a few – because if there was a complete list, everyone would run to their nearest axe shop, break into a theatre and massacre everyone – of the sort of stunts that actors in science-fiction films are capable of, the bastards.

1. STARING. Actors, contrary to public belief, do not spend all their time 'studying' their characters. If playing a famous person, they do not sit up all night with biographies of that person. Actors, in fact, are not generally academic. This is why they are always getting honorary degrees from the more publicity-crazed universities (see RECTORS). Because it's easier to become an actor and get a free degree than to be a student and do some proper work. Anyway, staring. This is the sort of thing that actors do instead of research. 'Aha,' says John or Jane Thesp, 'my character is from another world, I expect, I've never heard of this "Mercury" place. So therefore he won't blink! Because that's what aliens do! They don't blink!' And how does the actor know this? Because people do blink, and people aren't aliens, therefore … It saps your will to live, it really does.

2. TILTY-HEAD ACTING. Aliens are strange, right? They do unexpected things, like … be from another planet and that. So when you've done a good bit of staring, try this one. To indicate your alien nature and the fact that you find humans curious, tilt your head on one side and (this is the easy part) have a blank expression. Don't you look spooky!

3. THAT NECK-CRICKING THING. Film scholars must know where this gesture first appeared – the one where, after having beaten the knickers off some space soldiers, and been itself bashed up, or having fallen fifty floors into a skip, or anything where your alien, or robot, or villain has been a bit smashed up, he then gets up, walks down the road and then – wow! – uncricks his neck by tilting his head. He's such an alien! With a sense of humour.

4. THE DYING ROBOT SPEECH. Because even though the alien is the bad guy, and has shot everyone, including the hero's pet mice, he has to have a final scene where the audience realize that maybe he wasn't such a bad guy after all. And this generally means a speech. So cue either rain if outdoors, or wires sparking dangerously if indoors. Get your actor lying down, eyes half-open as though thinking of the ironies of life. Have them do a speech where – they – keep – stopping

— as life ebbs out of them. And end with the classic 'eyes suddenly staring upwards' bit. And then some dribbly liquid coming out of their mouth, because they're aliens.

5. NO EMOTIONS, EXCEPT FOR SOMETIMES. While it may seem easier for an actor to play something emotionless because then you don't actually have to be a good actor, this is in fact no fun for actor-boy. So every so often they just ignore the bloody script. There you are, 45 minutes into the movie, the robot alien villain has emotionlessly killed half the planet, when suddenly … the hero taunts the robot alien villain and he gets angry! That's an emotion! Or the robot, etc. finds a picture of a pretty girl, and tilts his head in an interesting and amusing way. Look, everyone! The robot fancies a picture of a girl! COME OFF IT!

SOAP-OPERA ACTING
〜

There are many clichés in this world and, being clichés, most of them are generally true. And one of the biggest clichés is that soap operas are rubbish (see *EASTENDERS*, *CORONATION STREET*, AUSTRALIAN SOAPS, AMERICAN SOAPS). Which, of course, is completely true. The other cliché is that, as it would logically follow, soap-opera acting is rubbish. Say it ain't so! It is so. These people really can't act. By some accident of fate – like being so fat it's funny, or being very good-looking but too stupid to be a model (imagine that!) – the actors in soap operas are actors in the same way a Bombay duck is a duck from Bombay.

Even on the rare occasion that a good actor ends up in a soap, the awfulness of the dialogue and plots and characterizations is such that soon they become rubbish. You see a good actor in a soap and that's not panic on his faces, that's his brain realizing what's going on and banging on the insides of his eyes trying to get help.

Here, for the record, are just a few of the many tricks the talentless flesh-wasters of soapland use to kill the hours before their next trip to the hip flask.

1. BEING QUIET. Soap actors watch real actors sometimes and many of them have noticed that real actors do not in fact shout and yell and stomp around. Often they are a bit moody and say things quietly. So your soaper has a go, and the results are always indifferent. 'Phil, I'm carrying your child, Phil!' 'Mumble mumble mumble.' 'Oh, Phil! I hoped you'd say that!'

2. BEING EMOTIONAL. Most soap actors, mind, take their cues from real opera. Possibly they think that 'soap operas' really are operas about soap. Be that as it may, soap actors do have a tendency to treat even the most piddling scene like it was the finale of the *Ring Cycle*. Buying a Mars Bar in the newsagent? Why not have an epileptic fit? Washing your hair when your cousin Bob comes in? Why, you're a handmaiden of Cleopatra and Bob a fierce Roman warrior. Standing in the background in a pub scene with no dialogue? You are a human bomb and nobody knows it – simmer with emotion and concealed gelignite!

3. BEING 'A COMICAL WOMAN'. This is an awful thing that happens mostly to northern actresses of a certain age. At a specific point in their career they stop being women and become, in effect, pantomime dames. Their accents develop into a fair approximation of the late Les Dawson in drag. And they become more hammy than the concept of ham itself.

4. BEING A HARD MAN. The tosser's route one to goal. Hard men are easy to act. All you have to do is not blink, wear a nasty leather coat and occasionally push someone so hard they almost move.

5. LEAVING THE SOAP. If they hate you, they will kill you (although natch, you can still come back, as a ghost or a zombie or just someone who forgot they were dead). And if they really hate you, they will kill you off-screen and your demise will be a brief line of insulting dialogue. 'Derek was killed in a bar for weirdos for being smelly.' But if you are lucky, you will get to leave the show alive, and on camera. There is only one way to do this. No matter what soap you are in, who your character is, or anything else, this is what happens. A taxi comes

to get you. You give them the address and then – instead of getting in like a normal person – you gaze around you, taking one last mental picture of the world you are leaving. Then, because you can't actually act, you do a sort of peculiar shudder in lieu of a real emotional reaction. Then you get in the cab and say, in a voice both shaky and determined (try this in front of the mirror first, you don't want to sound like Hitler in a rickshaw), 'Drive on.' Never fails.

BOY BANDS AND GIRL GROUPS
∾

Isn't it weird how boy bands are always a LOT wetter than girl groups? Because, possibly, girl bands are supposed to be 'feisty'. Ever since the Spice Girls invented Girl Power, which was basically feminism with all the politics, ideas and actual empowerment taken out, girl groups have always been a bit tougher than their male counterparts. Unlike boy bands, they can be seen drinking in clubs, having relationships with adults, and going out on the town. Boy bands are permanently cocooned in a world of pubescent innocence, only occasionally taking their tops off in videos and rubbing themselves with baby oil. It's all quite mystifying, really.

BOY BANDS AND GIRL GROUPS 2
∾

Apart from the obvious slur (they're all rent boys and slappers who can't sing), there are many bad things about boy bands and girl groups. But one slur that is false is, of course, that they've always been rubbish. 'Of course', even though not everyone seems to have noticed this.

Let's say this one more time. All music that isn't jazz, classical or 'world' is pop. That includes rock, soul, blues and all sorts. Which means that when you judge Led Zeppelin, you judge them not as members of a special magic category where they're as clever as jazz or as complex as classical music and so on. You judge them as pop. As in popular, popular music. The same with The Doors and the Rolling Stones and U2 and everyone.

So the best boy bands and girl groups are as good as the best rock bands, and also better than most rock bands full stop. Which means that, say, The Shirelles and The Supremes are in fact better than Slipknot, My Chemical Romance and Bon Jovi. The Monkees are better than just about everyone. Their manufacturedness is irrelevant. So is the fact that they didn't write their own songs. (Lots of groups should be encouraged not to write their own songs.) The end.

Of course, this would be an even stronger theory if there were any good boy bands other than The Monkees. Oh well, you can't have everything.

RINGTONES
∾

We already have a culture (see CULTURE) where ringtones are more popular than CDs (see COMPACT DISCS) because they are short, downloadable, and portable. Why stay at home listening to a gramophone or a music centre when you can walk around with your phone listening to the good bit (i.e. the most repeated bit) from your favourite song?

One day we will have a world where certain bits of songs will be the only thing that pop fans listen to. Just as once light classical fans enjoyed short, three-minute extracts from mighty symphonies, soon teenagers will just listen to three or four seconds out of some unmanageably long three-minute single. Compilation albums will be a few seconds long. The chart rundown, if there still is one, will just be some numbers followed by some sounds.

And this will continue, as these three-second samples are themselves shortened and sampled for further ringtones, while these microsecond ringtones will in turn be shortened, and so on, and so on … until one day all music will just be a sort of superfast blurty noise. Pop will blip itself.

RADIO STATIONS
∾

Instead of getting rid of the pirate stations in the 1960s and the 1990s, they should have banned all radio stations. Think what that would have done for creativity! Because if you wanted to be on the radio, instead of just writing to Radio One and saying, 'Hi! I am moderately attractive/grossly fat and I have done some hospital radio,' you'd have to fight for your right to be a DJ, possibly even shooting someone. Either that or we'd have Radio Four presenters broadcasting from the top of tower blocks and trying to do This Is Proper Culture shows with one broken microphone before the police arrive.

'Hi! This is Melvyn Bragg with – um – I had it written down – yeah, big up to the South Bank posse! Tonight's guests are Salman Rushdie and my girlfriend. But first I have to go to the toilet so chill to this dead air until I come back.'

Like that, really.

RADIO STATIONS 2

∾

Now we have this rotten 'narrowcasting' thing, as they used to call it, where, instead of big old stations that tried to encompass every aspect of our lives – you know, consumer shows, big-band music and plays – we now have stations that cater to the tiniest splinter in the finger of the market.

And it's not even like good old racist American radio, which ensures that different musical genres don't start having it off by keeping them in separate musical, as it were, boxes. In the US, you have country radio, hip-hop stations, indie and college, and that classic euphemism 'R'n'B', which just means 'black'. All the musics are kept in separate cells and only sometimes manage to communicate by banging tin cups against their bars.

But in Britain, we don't just divide music up by genre. We've gone a lot more Brave New World (see *BRAVE NEW WORLD*). We parcel it up by mood. Mellow FM. Light FM. Love FM. Relaxed FM. You can be sitting at home and think, Ooh, I feel slightly moody and very constipated – I think I'll put on Slightly Moody and Very Constipated FM. Ah, Razorlight, that's better.

DEATH OF THE MUSIC INDUSTRY

I t's not happy. Like all big spoiled brats, when the music industry is in trouble, it hollers its fat coked-up face off and tries to blame someone else. People aren't buying CDs! It's the fault of CD pirates! Well, you musical idiots, as any business person knows, supply is caused by demand, and your CDs were too dear. (There were never cassette bootleggers, and the vinyl bootleggers never caught on, so your CDs must have been hugely expensive.)

People aren't buying singles! Let's get rid of singles! Or let's maybe spend money on acts and write some original songs and things like that.

And the biggest whiny bleat of all: people are illegally downloading music! Rock bands are broke! Well, first of all one really, really doubts that Bono is going to have to go on the game to make some money anytime soon. And secondly, if you had the chance to bankrupt Sting, wouldn't you take it? Imagine: one day Celine Dion wakes up and there's an email for her saying, 'Dear Celine, nobody bought any of your CDs this month, goodbye.' Surely THAT'S worth fighting for?

DEATH OF THE MUSIC INDUSTRY 2

O h yeah, and while we're on the subject, this is the death of the music industry we're talking about. The terminal decline of one of the most corrupt, greedy, immoral and life-wrecking groups of people the world has ever seen. Boo hoo! Boo hoo!

VINYL

T hat black stuff they make 45 rpm and 33 rpm records out of. You feel sorry for vinyl. It doesn't know where to put itself at the moment. To elucidate, once upon a time life was easy for vinyl. It was, with the exception of cassettes (see CASSETTES), the only game in town. If you wanted to listen to music without using a radio or going to a concert, you either had to make it yourself, which could be risky, or you had to buy some vinyl.

At this point in history, there were no opinions about vinyl. Nobody said, 'Isn't it weird that we all listen to music by putting a metal arm with a needle on one end onto a rotating plastic disc? Doesn't that sound like something somebody might make up for a bet?' But so it was. Vinyl was unquestioned, possibly because it was loads better than some old wax with a big horn on one end.

Then vinyl was replaced, finally, by compact discs (see COMPACT DISCS). These were considered the future, and indeed they were the future, for about twenty years. Vinyl was out. People were saying, 'The sound quality of vinyl is no good, actually.'

Then, all of a sudden, people started saying, 'Actually, vinyl in some ways sounds better than a compact disc,' and spending loads of money on really expensive turntables. After that, MP3s came along (see MP3s) and then vinyl was even cooler, because there was a sleeve and a cover you could hold, and sleevenotes you could read and sometimes a little postcard.

So there we had it. Vinyl was everything, then it was rubbish, then it was cool. And now where are we? Vinyl is cool and does often sound nice and rich and full, but unfortunately it's still dirty great slices of plastic that go scratchy and get stuck and fluff gets on the needle which then goes VRVVVVVVV across the record and scratches it some more. And if you leave a record on the radiator, it turns into a Salvador Dalí copy of itself.

What we need are records made of solid diamond, although then we'd have to play them with needles made of superdiamonds.

CASSETTES
∽

Oddly maligned of late – well, not oddly at all, because there were many things wrong with them. But the idea that several large chains are going to get rid of cassettes just seems a bit brutal really, laying off the old workhorse just because it's not profitable. Cassettes, it would seem, are the donkeys of the music world, never particularly sexy or groovy, but quite good in their own way and certainly up for a lot of hard work.

So they hissed a bit? Well, maybe people should have recorded their songs a bit louder. Cassettes never hissed when you taped something absolutely deafening onto them. In fact, they seemed to have their own taste detector, allowing the likes of The Ronettes, The Clash and James Brown to thunder happily into the red, while letting Yes and Genesis and Pink Floyd noodle themselves into a sibilant dead end.

Apart from the hissing – and, yes, the fact that you had to spend seemingly hours fast-forwarding to the track you wanted and you could never get the exact start so you ended up listening to the end of the song you didn't like before the one you did like – cassettes were great. Except when they got a bit tense from overwork and made a strange wobbly WOOOMWOOM noise and you had to shake them until they came to their senses. Apart from those things, cassettes were great.

'Oddly maligned.'

CASSETTES 2

~

A nd compilations will never be the same. Like the LP, the home-made compilation tape had two sides, enabling the compiler to use their imagination and also to adhere to the classic principles of the narrative drama. Great compilation, or, as the hipsters call them, 'mixed' tapes, always followed certain rules. They would start optimistic, with a lively tune, move into a succession of cleverly (but not too cleverly) linked songs, and then, at the end of side one, ask, as it were a musical question, 'Do you want to carry on? ARE YOU READY FOR SIDE TWO?' If the answer was yes, and you hoped it was, side two would develop your main theme, chuck in a few quirky variants, perhaps have a Big Long Song, the mixed-tape equivalent of a soliloquy, and then lollop off into a tasteful conclusion.

You can't do that with an iTunes 'playlist'.

EASY CLASSICAL MUSIC VERSUS DIFFICULT CLASSICAL MUSIC

~

O h, where to begin? The whole debate about easy classical music is based on not one, but two types of snobbery. The first snobbery is an easy one. It says that people who like easy classical music – you know the sort of thing: stuff with tunes, stuff from adverts and films, and so on – are some sort of baboon-like idiots. They like their music the way a baby likes its dinner, mashed up and blended and smoothed into a paste that even the most toothless pre-infant could digest.

This is true. But there is also a simple riposte to that argument. So. Flaming. What. One doesn't recall Beethoven and Bach and Mozart sitting down one afternoon – and yes, they did live at different times, it's called a Hypothetical Example, Mister Classical Pants – anyway, Ludwig and JS and Wolfgang didn't get together one afternoon in Der Alte Starbucks and say, 'Right, here are the rules of classical music. One, it should be difficult. Two, it should be no fun. And three, only people who can play the bass viol are allowed to like it.'

Here is one of the golden rules of life:

PEOPLE CAN LIKE WHATEVER THEY LIKE AND THAT'S FINE.

Really. That applies to religion, sex, golf, Phil Collins, everything. So long as nobody else gets hurt (i.e. fleeing from the room as soon as 'Against All Odds' comes on the stereo and banging your shin), it doesn't matter. So if your Auntie Maisie or your bank manager or a chubby little cub scout professes a liking for a bit of tuneful classical music, THEY ARE NOT SERIAL KILLERS.

EASY CLASSICAL MUSIC VERSUS DIFFICULT CLASSICAL MUSIC 2
∾

And what's wrong with a sodding tune anyway?

EASY CLASSICAL MUSIC VERSUS DIFFICULT CLASSICAL MUSIC 3
∾

Oh yeah, that second snobbery thing. It's true that all the serious classical buffs are complete knobstones about their music and think that everyone who doesn't prefer a pound of raw Bartok to Mozart's theme from *Chorlton and the Wheelies* is a stupid fool. And it's bad, too, for reasons stated above.

But equally vexing is the snobbery of people who like easy classical music. They say, 'I don't see why they have to have all those boring bits' as though Tchaikovsky sat down one day and thought, Hmm, this 1812 Overture is a bit exciting, I'll give them 45 minutes of boring bits to pad it out. Should someone actually use a word like 'contrapuntal', they say 'I don't like all that fancy jargon', misusing the word 'jargon' to mean 'essential vocabulary of the job'.

And they really, really, really do wish that classical music – and all music – had stopped in 1901. Life would be so much easier if the police had gone round Sir Edward Elgar's house the day he finished writing Land of Pomp and Circumstance, or whatever it's called, taken it off him and said, 'Right, that's it. From now on, no more music. We'll have wars and the internal combustion engine instead.'

But music continued, and got a bit weird, and then black people got involved, and saxophones, and it all got a bit DIFFICULT.

EASY CLASSICAL MUSIC VERSUS DIFFICULT CLASSICAL MUSIC 4
❧

And another thing. Why does everybody who likes 'nice' classical music only want it in little bits? Three minutes from 'The Four Seasons'. The advert bit from the 'New World Symphony'. The climax to John Cage's '4.33'. Could it be that they have the attention spans of rap-loving teenagers? Do they have a tendency to wander into the garden during the longer sections of 'Carmina Burana'?

We may never know. But the weird thing is that, proportionately, cutting classical music into little chunks is like enjoying pop music in short, five-second bursts. Which makes listening to music like being at a pop quiz. 'Okay, now it's the classical music round. We're going to play ten great classical pieces, divided into nice three-minute chunks, and you have to identify them. That's one point for the composer, one point for the name of the piece, and three points if you can identify which episode of *Brideshead Revisited* it was used in.'

JAZZ
❧

Jazz involves a very special kind of snobbery, one where you totally get to choose what you are going to be snobbish about. Because 'jazz' as a term is extremely wide. It can mean some men in bowler hats playing very jolly tunes, or it can mean some men in berets playing miserable things, or it can mean women in black dresses singing songs about shagging in front of a double bass, or it can mean dancing to bands who know far too many notes … Jazz isn't so much a broad church as a church that has to book two seats on an aeroplane and gets sweaty just walking to the hot-dog stand.

Which means that you can – brilliantly if you're a music snob – like jazz and totally hate it at the same time. This does happen in other genres, but not with such intensity. True, rock fans often despise pop, but not to the exclusion of all else. Classical fans do tend to divide on the old Stockhausen versus Mozart bit but most of them do agree that, say, Beethoven is all right.

But jazz fans! Blimey, they're like those Japanese fish. The ones that eat each other if placed in the same tank. Only with berets on. Give a trad jazz fan a bebop record and he'll tell you that Charlie Parker murdered jazz. Give a woman in a black dress a trad jazz record and she'll say it sounds like some embarrassing old dads.

Will jazz never find peace?

INDIE MUSIC
∾

The long version: indie music used to be a term that described people with no money making records without the control and influence of the mainstream music industry. These days, indie bands are mostly in it for the trilbies. There is no sense of smashing the system, changing the world or even rebelling against anything other than people who don't wear little trilbies.

INDIE MUSIC 2
∾

The short version: indie music is people who haven't got any problems singing about their problems.

KARAOKE
∾

Please stop it now. Not just because karaoke is an awful thing to witness when you're having a quiet drink and some throatbungler gets up on his or her enormous haunches and starts to hammer nails into the head of a song that you once loved. That's not the half of it. No, what's happened with karaoke is that it now infuses every aspect of our entertainment culture. You can't turn on the television without seeing someone who 'learned' to sing from getting up at karaoke and ramming their vile tongues down the throat of some poor innocent tune.

'Please stop it now.'

KARAOKE 2

∽

A nd what's really bad is that once upon a time people learned music at their grandpa's knee, or from their older siblings' record collection, or in church. Now people learn their music from a catalogue. A grubby, looseleaf catalogue with the pages sealed in muggy transparent plastic like the menu in the worst musical takeaway in the sewers below hell.

'RETURN TO FORM'

∽

T he record reviewer's classic lazy escape clause. When faced, as is increasingly common these days, with a record by some really old man or a band who have been around since the 1960s, the sensible reaction is to throw the thing into a nearby furnace. People who've been around that long might be fun to go and see live but rarely have the creative spark intact, if sparks can stop being intact. So what was once a joyous occasion – the release of a new album by Legendary 60s Blokey – is now cause for hiding under the bed.

But every so often charity hits the cruel heart of the cynical journo. After all, wasn't this bloke once our hero? Didn't he reshape popular music? And there's a song on this album that's not too totally awful. Also, the producer has made sure that the single sounds a bit like one of blokey's good songs from the old days. Plus the reviewer is a bit pissed.

So the review is written, and towards the end, maybe in the last line, are the three dreaded words: 'return to form'. Oh dear. Someone's going to buy that album because of you, you know.

RAP

∽

I n the old days we used to hate it when DJs talked over records, particularly if they were on Radio One and had stupid beards and talked like an educated wasp ('Annnnnd nwww, the nnnew single frrrrm …). Nowadays it seems that nearly all music consists of people talking over records, while ironically the actual records are played by a DJ who never says anything. Perhaps it's meant to be a sort of hell for DJs, where Dave Lee Travis finds himself playing music which is, like, supposed to be his JOB, but he's unable to talk because he can't get a word in over MC Shut Up Dave Lee Travis.

In the world of hip-hop, grime, two step, hardbag, hyphy, crunk and, quite possibly, strictly ballroom dancing on ice, the song has long been replaced by what your granny now knows is called 'rapping'. Of course, the trendy kid round the corner who buys the *NME* because none of the other kids will let him join their gangs calls rapping 'rhyming' or 'spitting', but that's just so people don't mistake him for your granny.

The cruel part for a generation of rock dads who liked to go around saying, 'You can't hear the words and there's no tune,' is that a) you can hear the words, very clearly, which can be embarrassing in mixed company, and b) even though there is no tune, nobody will understand you when you say that because these days 'tune' just means 'a record I like'. Which is why at Sting concerts, when people leap up and shout 'tune', they mean, 'I liked that!', not 'Write something with a tune!'

HIP HOP

~

So-called purely and entirely to make codgers and jazz fans go round saying, 'What exactly is the difference between rap and hip hop?' AARGH!

HIP HOP 2

~

The major currency of popular music in the twenty-first century. Really. All your Pink Floyds and Rolling Stones and Joni Mitchells fade into a pleasant sort of woollen grey next to the ridiculous force and popularity of hip hop. It's so popular that people who don't like it know about it. It has infiltrated every area of modern life. There are hip-hop movies, hip-hop books, hip-hop barbers and, quite probably, hip-hop accountants (there certainly are hip-hop judges, as none of the buggers seem capable of delivering a simple judgment – see PEOPLE WHO LIKE BEING TAKEN SERIOUSLY – without doing so in the form of a lame 50 Cent impression).

Its popularity among 'young people' is understandable; like rock 'n' roll, punk and acid house, rap is rebel music that your parents will almost certainly not like (unless of course they are under 30, in which case, kids, really annoy them by getting into light opera. If you can stand it.) And it's easy to assimilate. All you need to do is buy some pretend gold, get a backing track and you can make any old noise and you'll still be better than Westlife.

In the future, of course, rap's popularity will fade and its perceived complexity derided. Young people will find solace in the simpler, less virtuoso music of Freddie and the Dreamers, the most genuinely scary band in the history of pop.

JOSEPH AND THE AMAZING TECHNICOLOR DREAMCOAT VERSUS JESUS CHRIST SUPERSTAR

∿

Whatever the musical merits of either of them (and certainly these are the shows where most of the tunes are buried, Lloyd-Webber-wise), the most bizarre thing about them is the way they reverse the traditional attitudes of the Old and New Testaments. Thus Joseph, which is part of the Old Testament – that bloodbath of vengeance, fury, commandments, plagues, fire and sin – is a sunny dayglo romp for all the family. Whereas the story of Christ – taken from the New Testament, the biblical home of love, forgiveness and redemption – is turned into a horrific nightmare of guilt, neurosis, misery and doubt.

In fact, this principle seems to apply to pretty much all of Lloyd-Webber's work (see *PHANTOM OF THE OPERA*). Eva Peron? In the musical, a saint. In real life, a prozzie married to a nasty old bloke. *Starlight Express*? In the musical, a lot of happy dancers pretending to be trains. In real life, a transport accident waiting to happen.

Only *Cats* is what it says it's about. A bunch of bastards.

PHANTOM OF THE OPERA
~

A handy yardstick for people who can't tell opera from musicals. The *Phantom of the Opera* isn't an opera, it's about an opera. It's also crap.

BAND REUNIONS
~

Not a good idea. Partly because bands split up for a reason (i.e. they hate each other), and partly because they take place so long after the original event that, when the band come onstage, instead of seeing a fresh-faced quartet of cheeky pop lads (see LADS), the audience reel in horror as four hideous golems with musical instruments assemble, clearly for the purpose of killing everyone in the room.

Worst of all are those chilling words uttered by the singer at the press conference: 'If things go well with the tour, we're going to record a new album.' No! Not that! Anything but that!

ACADEMIES FOR THE PERFORMING ARTS
~

Or 'schools of rock'. Or 'stage school for the sort of people who really shouldn't go within a million miles of stage school'. It's bad enough having kids taught how to sing selections from *Annie* when they should be learning maths and so on, but teaching popular music is appalling. Just when you thought music couldn't get any politer, eh?

'No! Not that! Anything but that!'

ARTS & MEDIA

TABLOIDS

❧

Despite their screaming headlines, nudity and salaciousness, they're also deeply Victorian. For example, whenever there's an article or a news piece about binge drinking in the paper (see BINGE DRINKING), it's always accompanied by a picture of a woman looking snozz-faced, not a man. This is presumably because a woman who drinks herself stupid is somehow a more shocking thing than a man who is blind stonkered. It's a throwback to a Victorian view of the world, where women were supposed to sit at home and sew samplers that read I WANT TO KILL MYSELF instead of going out every night and having a good, if vomity, time.

Their whole morality is deeply odd. They pay lip service to all kinds of modern things – gay weddings, anti-racism, television – but you sense that they don't really approve. They're like an old, smelly vicar who's been told to be nice to the gays but is really waiting for things to change so he can damn them all to hell.

POSH TABLOIDS

❧

The spivs of the newspaper world, posh tabloids pretend to be real newspapers (and so, sometimes, do real newspapers). They have long names, often with the word *Daily* in them. They have serious typefaces and they refer to members of the Royal Family by their titles, rather than by their nicknames. They have editorials and columns by people who don't have nice hair and pretty chests. But deep down, these newspapers are really a bit common. They long to go out for some fish and chips and a bottle of stout, maybe see a flick and pick up a tart. Add that to their strange obsessions with sex crimes and right-wing politics and the only conclusion possible is that if these papers were a person, they'd be serving time for doing someone in under Brighton Pier.

CELEBRITY MAGAZINES

~

False advertising, by and large. A fishing magazine has lots of fish in it, interviews with fishermen and pictures of fishermen and fish and fishing rods. A stamp magazine is the same, only with stamps and stamp collectors. But a celebrity magazine? There are two things to take into account with celebrities and celebrity magazines.

1. **There are never any celebrities in celebrity magazines.** There are just photographs of celebrities, usually taken from a long way away, and articles about celebrities written by people who aren't celebrities and padded out with quotes from experts who aren't celebrities either (see TALKING HEADS).

2. **Sometimes you do see celebrities in celebrity magazines.** These are rubbish celebrities. They are famous for being in celebrity magazines and as such always look a bit confused, as they are very much fish out of water. Their natural home is perhaps teaching a dance class, or male prostitution, yet here they are helping to fill up the pages of a celebrity magazine. It's like asking a horse to type.

FREE NEWSPAPERS

~

Those ones that unhappy people with funny trolleys give out in the street. They are absolutely rubbish. There's no news in them. Or rather, there's no *new* news in them. They just copy the news from other, more proper newspapers, and that's the front page sorted. The rest is just pictures of 'celebrities' getting out of cars, reviews written by people who've never written anything more than their names before, and some adverts. They are a cross between *Heat* magazine and some sort of free brochure you get at the zoo, advertising some other zoos.

ART

The whole thing has just changed these last few decades. Used to be a time when art was a means of communication. Literally. Here's a picture of a goat. Here's Caveman Len killing the goat. Everyone say, 'Well done, Caveman Len! You killed a goat!' And it went on like that for hundreds and thousands of years. Here's Jesus having a word with some men. It's meant to illustrate some bit of the Bible. In the background is some weird stuff, like deer and fish and a wheel, but it's not meant to be weird. The deer and the fish and the wheel would all be specific symbols with meanings readily accessible to people.

And more years go by. Ophelia in a lake. Rodin's Thinker. Tchaikovsky's 'Symphonie Pathetique'. All, you know, meant to communicate, like, stuff.

And art was oddly accessible. Sometimes so much so that going to an art gallery was like entering the world's easiest GUESS WHAT THIS IS MEANT TO BE competition. There would be a painting, or a statue, of a goddess crying. And underneath, a caption that read, 'THE GODDESS CRIES'. Ten points!

Lately, though, art has not been designed to communicate. Stun, shock, entertain, yes, but not communicate. This is not to say that it's necessarily bad, but if it's only comprehensible to a small group of, say, one person, then what's the point? Eh? You can't hear the words and there's no tune. And the portions are so small. And so on.

ART 2

Of course, it's all about money now (yeah, like in the past artists worked for free and spurned all payment). The best way to deal with artists is to pay them with a cheque for a million wrens and a picture of Tuesday. That way, when they say, 'Hey, not that I care about money, but we agreed on a proper fee, not this wrens and Tuesday rubbish,' you can say, 'It may be rubbish to you, but to me this cheque makes perfect sense.' WOOONNNN-NIL! WOOOONNN-NIL!

BOOK INTRODUCTIONS
∾

There are two types of introduction. One is quite useful. It goes like this:

'Hello, my name is Frederick. What is your name?'

This is good because it is polite, informative and helpful. It also saves you doing all this sort of nonsense:

'I'm terribly sorry, I remember the face but I'm awfully bad at remembering names. Who the hell are you?'

Or:

'My name's Jim. And you are? And you are ... and ... TELL ME YOUR NAME, DAMN YOU!'

The other kind of introduction is in no way useful at all. It is called a book introduction and, unlike the other sort of introduction, is completely pointless. For a start, all the information you might want to know about the book should be contained in the author's biography. And if that's not informative enough, there's the preface (see PREFACES), and if you're still crazed with a lust for information, why not fast-forward to the acknowledgements or pause the book on the footnotes (see ACKNOWLEDGEMENTS and FOOTNOTES)?

The reason the introduction is there is twofold:

1. **To get a famous person to plug the book.** This makes you look more famous by association and also makes you look like you know some famous people. The problem with this is that famous people are generally too 'busy' to read – i.e. they can't read. So an introduction by a famous person normally goes something like this:

I have known Jimmy X for some time. When he asked me to write the introduction to this book I was delighted. Books are nice. Thank you.

2. The other reason for including an introduction is, essentially, to show off. This sort of introduction tends to cack on and on about the circumstances in which the book was written, mentions all the people whose ideas you stole to write it, has a useless joke about your wife doing the typing or being patient or something lying and made-up like that, and frequently ends with a completely pointless name-checking of the place where the book was written. Boiled down to three words, all this introduction says is: 'Look at ME!'

PREFACES
∾

Probably as different to introductions (see INTRODUCTIONS) as donkeys are to asses. Prefaces seem to be allowable if, by some fluke, the book has been reprinted or has achieved 'classic' status (i.e. it was made into a bad film with British actors in it (see ACTORS). Thus the author is allowed to reminisce about the times when the book was written, the changes it wrought on the world (and he or she will use the word 'wrought') and how, from their position of near-senescence, they lament a changing world. In reality, everything a preface says can be summed up in three words: 'Look at ME!'

ACKNOWLEDGEMENTS
∾

A great way of showing off. Having a list of acknowledgements – the books you nicked ideas out of to write your book, the people you interviewed and the name-droppingly famous people who 'offered me advice' and 'encouraged me when all seemed dark' – is yet another way to say three little words: 'Look at ME!'

FOOTNOTES
∾

The mud of literature. There you are reading a book when suddenly there's a sodding little number 1 or a small star or a tiny sword next to a word. And before you can stop yourself, your eye is drawn down to the bottom of the page. Where you will find, not a raunchy picture or a splendid joke, but the most boring fact you have ever read. And this will go on through the rest of the book. Footnotes are the literary equivalent not just of someone being interrupted as they are telling a story, but of someone interrupting *themselves* as they tell a story. In other words, only a mental person would do footnotes.

AUTHOR BIOGS

The picture's always wonky. The photographer only gets a namecheck if he or she is really, really famous. The facts about the writer are massaged to make them look more famous. And, if there are no massageable facts, they are forced to put in, as a last resort, stuff that no one cares about.

Jimmy X was born in Leicester in 1978. He attended WHO GIVES A TOSS School and graduated from SO WHAT College in 2000; AND DEAR GOD, I'M ON THE EDGE OF MY SLEEP HERE.

That sort of thing.

INDEXES

An index is the easiest and simplest way of determining a book's quality. If a book has an index – and many fine books don't, of course – then a quick look at it will tell the casual reader just how good the book is.

If, for example, the index is massive, deeply complicated and has entries like this:

Cawnpore, Lord: born in a hammock in India, pp. 3–27; educated by Thuggee, pp. 34–65; eaten by mice, pp. 78–92; becomes Prime Minister, pp. 87–97

the chances are it is a well-researched, substantial sort of book. If however, the index is a bit brief, has a very large typeface and looks like this:

Marsh, Jodie: buys a hat, p. 6; buys another one, p. 6

then it's probably not very good and your best bet is to look at the pictures in the shop and put it back on the shelf with all jammy fingerprints on it.

JANE AUSTEN

Yes, she's quite funny. Yes, she's a bit sarcastic. Yes, she accidentally wrote some quite good Sunday night telly. But flaming Nora, a little bit of Jane Austen goes a long way. The constant snarkiness, for a start. You can't say hello to a Jane Austen heroine without her saying, 'And, pray, is that what passes for manners in Bath these days?' The epigrams, which take about four days to set up for fairly small reward. 'It is a truth universally acknowledged, that a single man in possession of a good –' GET ON WITH IT!

JANE AUSTEN 2

And the plots are all the bloody same. Girl is unpopular because everyone else is a dick. Girl is clever, especially compared to everyone else. Girl can't get a bloke, probably because she's so bastard rude to everyone all the time. Girl meets bloke. Girl is rude to bloke. Bloke buggers off. Girl pretends she doesn't care. Bloke is apparently marrying someone else. Girl realizes she does care. Bloke not marrying someone else after all. Girl meets bloke, sort of apologizes. Bloke marries girl. Girl's stupid ugly family are amazed. The end.

> 'Yes, she accidentally wrote some quite good Sunday night telly. But flaming Nora, a little bit of Jane Austen goes a long way.'

Oh, and apparently she never mentioned the Napoleonic Wars. (Nor did Shakespeare, but at least he had a reason.) This is a shame because, goodness, the Napoleonic Wars would have livened up Jane Austen's books no end.

'And, pray, is that what passes for manners in Bath these days?'
BOOM! BANG! EXPLOSION!

THE BRONTES
~

Why are there so many of them? Which books did they write?
Why do their TV adaptations never seem as much fun as Jane
Austen's and Charles Dickens' (see JANE AUSTEN and CHARLES
DICKENS)? Is it because the Brontes (and we'll be having none of
your fancy Yorkshire umlauts here, thankee) are, like Haribos, only
good when served by the pound? Probably.

CHARLES DICKENS
~

Probably the most adapted male author in the world, Dickens is, if
you will, the twinkly Victorian dad to Jane Austen's ironic Geor-
gian mum. But where Austen only ever did annoying waspish books
about annoying waspish women who were rude to perfectly pleasant
men in funny trousers, Dickens was more varied. That is, he started
off writing jolly books about jolly people who drank porter and ate
pies and had names like Mister Whimsicrank. Then he wrote lots of
sentimental old codge about orphans who were rescued from the snow
by pickpockets and had names like Tim Ogglers. And finally, he
became a very glum writer of long, dour books where nothing much
happened and everyone wore black and had names like Mrs Frizzle-
coffin. In fact, Dickens seems to have access to some sort of early
computer, so clearly are his characters' names the product of some
Charles Dickens' Character Name Generator. (And those are the good
ones. The rest of the time he seems to have given his characters names
that were just descriptions of their personality, like Lord Richgreedyfat
or Dickie Beerliking.)

Dickens' books are a terrifying combination of tweeness, sentiment
and hangings. They perfectly complement and mirror the Victorian
era. Which is why we shouldn't have to put up with them now. We
don't travel by horse and carriage or wear crinolines or die of

'Lots of sentimental old codge about orphans who were rescued from the snow by pickpockets and had names like Tim Ogglers.'

consumption any more, so why should we read some crumply old daddy's book tat? More to the point, why should we endure it on the telly? Hours and hours of people you quite liked in a *Harry Potter* film wearing bonnets and whiskers and saying, 'Indeed, Captain Fusskettle' in a stupid wheezy voice.

JAMES BOND
❧

He's back, you know. No he isn't! It's not him! James Bond, we read in the nicer papers, is an 'archetype', a legendary figure who takes the place of the mythic heroes of yore, and all that toot. His tenure in the human psyche will last forever, as attested to by his continuing presence in la dee da dee blah dee blah.

Anyone who, having passed the age of fifteen, reads a James Bond novel now (and why are they always called 'novels', like they were by Anthony Trollope or someone) will be not so much struck by as beaten up and stuffed into a coal cellar by how ... well, how silly they are.

Never mind all this 'male wish fulfilment' stuff, Ian Fleming writes Bond like a mad shopping fantasy. He is the adult(ish) equivalent of a little girl writing to Father Christmas. Except Fleming is more 'Dear Santa, for Xmas I would like an Aston Martin and some Martinis and cigars too and also a gun! – a Walther PPK because they are the best and a jetpack and a Bentley and some girls please, but later can they be shot because girls are not nice.'

And then there's the sex. As far as can be made out, James Bond's idea of a rude night out is having it off with a woman who, from her name, is in reality probably a trannie; then being kidnapped and having his goolies whipped. All a bit suspect, when you think about it, and probably a desperate substitution device for his very pressing real wants. Any half-decent agony aunt would tell you that what James Bond really needs is a boyfriend.

'FANTASY'

Literature is a wonderful thing. It comes in many forms, too, most of which are pretty good. But there is one aspect of literature that would try the patience of a saint, even a particularly well-tempered saint with no personal problems who never gets hangovers. And that branch is 'fantasy' literature.

Even the phrase is annoying, because fantasy is generally written by people who can barely write their own names, let alone those of the Five Lords of the Outer Nathganoggy. And yet these are the people most drawn to fantasy literature. It's all a bit unfair, really. The bars and cheap hotels of the world are full of mute, inglorious Miltons, men and women who never quite got that literary break, whereas the bookshops of the world are crammed with big, chunky, sequel-faced editions of horrible, awful, rotten books about trolls and warriors by people who write like they are chewing the alphabet with their mouth open.

But let us leave aside the cacky prose style of the fantasy writer for a moment. The whole idea of the Fantasy Novel is deeply repellent in the first place. Even science fiction (see SCIENCE FICTION) has a point; it reflects, albeit in a geekatronic sort of way, the hopes and fears mankind has for the future, and on a good day gives us new ways of thinking about the present (on a bad day it makes you want to hand the book to your robot butler for shredding). Romantic fiction, whodunnits, airport novels, even all of these have virtues – insight into the human condition, suspense, the feeling of sheer criminal joy you get on eating a pound of junk food. But none of this applies to fantasy.

For a start, the stories are all rubbish. They do not, as some advertise, tap into the mythos of human existence. They are, resonance-wise, not so much Joseph Campbell as *Joseph and His Amazing Technicolor Dreamcoat*. And nearly all of them are nicked from *Lord of the Rings*. This, as it happens, is where the trouble started. J.R.R. 'Look Who's' Tolkien was a proper professor, who read proper legends in the original Anglo-Saxon and based his tales of hairy-footed midgets and fairy women with Mr Spock ears on research. All right, it was research into made-up stuff, but at least it was made-up stuff from thousands of years ago. Tolkien's fiction was rooted in the very fabric of legends' beginning. Not in a long night's session playing WarChampion online in your boxer shorts.

And it's a bit … well, gay. Not 'gay' as in homosexual but gay as in 'prat'. (And see 'GAY'.) There's something a bit odd about all these warrior blokes who are all muscular and wear skimpy pants and no shirts, and hang around with elven ladies a lot but never have sex with them. Mind you, if fantasy novelists were actually gay, they'd give all the warriors great big trouser-filling … anyway. Fantasy is 'gay', but not gay.

Oh, nearly forgot – the prose style of fantasy novels. Also 'gay', as it consists entirely of either chewy sentences *a la* a ten-year-old boy's first story, like this: 'Grimgot gazed up at the hideous wizard prince lord, his mighty muscles hiding his fear and awe of the Clan Leopard-Wasp.' Or it's loads of really duff dialogue doubly hampered by a deep-seated fear of the word 'said'. '"Nonsense!" roared Jar-Niflik' or '"Why, what foolery is this," laughed Hagspoon mightily.'

'Gay'.

SCIENCE FICTION

Science fiction used to be great. Well, before that it actually used to be nonsense. Books about science fiction – which you can only get out of the library if you've had the word NERDULON tattooed on your actual face – always tend to start with Greek mythology or Leonardo Da Vinci or any fool in a robe who imagined 'engines of flight' or people whose torsos had faces in them and so on. Now these are, frankly, not the sort of thing that George Lucas could make a career out of (although lately a few Jedi Torsos With Faces In Them would be preferable to his recent output, eh, film fans?) but when your imagination is forced to rely on things like spears and amphoras as building blocks, then nobody can really be said to be at fault. And so, time passed, and when some real things had been invented, like steam trains and the Spinning Jenny, we started to get Proper Science Fiction.

And that was pretty exciting. Submarines shaped like giant herrings! That were being attacked by enormous squids! Moon rockets made out of old cricket bats and railings! Men on the Moon! Wearing diving suits and being attacked by eight-armed green-skinned men! Called the Morgulators! Sex! Although, to be honest, it wasn't so much sex as blonde women called Wenn-Dii looking on admiringly as some chump in an inventor's hat showed them the secrets of man's red accountancy.

Science fiction developed apace and got so exciting that real life started to copy it. Moon landings, nuclear bombs and TV shows where people had sex and they showed it all become commonplace. So what did science fiction do then? It let us down, that's what it did. As with robots – and jetpacks, and food pills, and having fins like a shark on the shoulder-pads of your jacket – science fiction dropped the ball. It had a big sulk because the real world was better at being weird than it was.

And so science fiction became depressing. It became doomy. Instead of saying, 'Hey, kids! The future's going to be absolutely brilliant! Let's all put on bikinis and dance on the Sun!', it decided to say, 'Not to worry anybody, but the way things are going, what with global warming and surveillance and that big grey mushy tide of nanobytes thing, the future is going to be absolutely horrible.'

So thanks for that, science fiction. You've really ruined our day.

DETECTIVE NOVELS

∾

Sherlock Holmes is all right, despite the fact that Arthur Conan Doyle thought, You know what? It's rubbish inventing the greatest detective in the history of fiction and totally setting the standard for all detective novels hereafter. I think I'll jack that in and start believing in fairies instead.

Miss Marple and Hercule Poirot are quite good, although with Poirot you can never actually remember which one of them you've read and you have to look at the ending to see which it was. And Miss Marple is inadvertently responsible for inventing *Murder She Wrote*, which is not only a bloody awful TV show but also enabled loads of boring people at parties to say, 'Actually, they should arrest Angela Lansbury because wherever she goes, someone gets murdered, snorf snorf ha ha!'

Apart from that, all detective stories are rubbish. This is because a) they're all rubbish, and b) they all feature a Flawed Hero. Flawed Heros are all the same. They're all incredibly good at their job – which is always being a detective, because nobody wants to read a novel about a Flawed Building Society Manager – but they all have a Flaw, which is generally that their wife died, or they used to be a serial killer, or something like that. And, just to make it worse, they also have an Interesting Side to Them. Which is usually poetry, although it can be

'All detective stories are rubbish.'

anything from collecting samurai swords or knowing a lot about vases. Either way, these people should be presenting *Antiques Roadshow*, not trying to solve murders.

And you can always work out the ending with this simple formula. It's never the most likely one, or the least likely one, or the one who got killed halfway through. Unless it is, in which case that's not the author being clever, she just got pissed halfway through writing chapter seven and forgot.

TECHNOLOGY &
NEW THINGS

MYSPACE

~

The phenomenon of the age. More than YouTube or 'blogs' (see YOUTUBE and BLOGS), MySpace is the lynchpin of the modern internet. If you've just been successfully revived from cryogenic storage, you may not know how MySpace works. It is basically a big old vanity board, where you can put up everything about yourself that you can think of. And then other equally vain people write to you, and you all write to each other and it's a scream. You wonder how anybody gets any work done these days, you really do.

A typical MySpace page generally contains three or more of the following things:

1. **A 'funny' photo, generally of the page user looking mad.** Or, if they are a Goth, looking at the camera from a funny angle.

2. **Some music, if they're a musician, or want to be.** If they really, really want to be a musician, there will be a little bit too much music.

3. **A lot of lists that you don't care about.** Favourite films. 'Influences'. Friends. After about nine pages of this wallowing in self-promotion, you just want to go, 'I don't KNOW you!' Biographies of Napoleon are less detailed than these things. Railway timetables are less informative.

4. An even worse list, this time of people who want to be the page user's friend. This is worse because there seems to be no limit to the amount of 'funny' pictures people can take of themselves. And the messages! 'Hi! Great gig!' and 'Missed you last night' and a forest of inanity. If this is the stuff that people feel compelled to post online,

imagine how grim and boring their conversations face to face in the pub must be.

5. A 'blog' (see BLOGS). This is actually the only indicator of how famous or not the page user is. If it's really detailed and there are new entries every day, they're not famous. If there's about one entry a year, they're quite well-known. If someone else writes it for them, they're famous.

MYSPACE 2

MySpace has also been responsible, in a slightly dubious and definitely unproved way, for helping along the careers of some new young pop acts. This is entirely possible – after all, if you could download someone's music for free even if you hadn't heard it (and if it was Morrissey, especially if you hadn't heard it), then that would surely be more appealing than paying for some music on a CD that you hadn't heard.

But, beyond that, it all seems a bit duff. For a start, with all the messageboards and chatting and LET'S MEET BEFORE THE GIG IN RHYL, it's just too easy. Yes, easy. Half the fun of being a teen pop fan was the difficulty of finding any good music. The bands on MySpace are the kind of people who, once, would have turned up to do a gig in your bedroom. Far too easy, and whiffing very strongly of 'publicity stunt'. And, in the case of many of the acts who come to prominence via a massive internet fanbase, it turns out a) that a big record company has put them on the Net to make them look slightly less uncool, and b) they were rubbish. So there.

FACEBOOK

It's the new MySpace, or it was last week. Yet another page where you send emails to people you already know and ask them to be your friend, even though if you've got their email addresses, presumably they're your friends already, or at least some kind of acquaintance.

Maybe you fell out with them and this is a way of building bridges. Maybe not.

The worst thing about these pages is the incessant chatter of people you hardly know gabbing on and on about stuff you don't care about. 'Alan Westmoreland has changed his relationship status.' What to? BORING AND SINGLE? 'You have been invited to join the "I Like Spangles Discussion Group".' Oh, thanks! No, really! Thanks ever so!

The only difference between Facebook and all the other yackety crappety places is that it's apparently more middle class. So that's all right then.

YOUTUBE

∾

One of the rockier yet also more floral outcrops of modern life, YouTube is a classic example of something that just wasn't there a year or two ago and now seems to be ridiculously prevalent. Like everything on the internet (see THE INTERNET), it has the potential to be brilliant – and sometimes it is – yet it is generally used for the most banal thingamajigs.

The idea, lest you have recently escaped from Saint Helena, is a simple one. You make videos and YouTube will show them, for free. It is a lovely concept. Unless these videos are rude, anything goes. And some people do make the effort, with short films and rants and animation and all that. It's like a tiny arts centre, only it didn't come off the council tax so the *Daily Mail* can't have a go at it.

But most of its users just put up pop videos. Or bits of telly. Or film of their mate Aaron falling off his skateboard. It's classic internet usage. If someone found a way to communicate with space aliens and put it on the Net, within two days the site would be filled with messages like ALIENS R GAY and THIS IS AARON HE FELL OF HIS SKATEBOARD, OW.

And the messages! Half of them are by people who clearly find texting too complex (see TEXT MESSAGING). Several are just plain vile. And most of them are, well, not too sharp. Underneath the video, you generally find someone's written 'WHAT IZ THIS?' – right next to the maker's detailed explanation of, um, what it is. It's like a chat room for the deeply slow (see CHAT ROOMS). All right, they're mostly only twelve, but so was Mozart. And he wouldn't have posted episode 532 of Pokemon. Not without writing a proper theme song, and an opera.

FRIENDS REUNITED
∾

Some people don't ever cotton on to the fact that there's a reason people frequently don't maintain friendships after they leave school. In fact, there are three reasons:

1. **That was school.** You're not reading *The Blue Pirate* and *Penelope the Pink Car* any more, so why would you be hanging out with little Jimmy from Year 2?

2. **You have to have a friendship in the first place before you can resume one.**

3. **People don't always 'drift apart'.** Sometimes they run like hell.

BLOGS
∾

'**B**log' is apparently short for 'weblog', which tells you nothing about modern life except that the whole process of coining abbreviations has totally gone to pot. Using this process, the abbreviations for, say, 'travel agent', 'chip shop' and 'silly abbreviation' would be 'lagent', 'pshop' and 'yabbreviation', the last one sounding oddly accurate.

Anyway, 'blogging' is one of the most popular internet activities there is, which tells you everything about the awful and pessimism-led fate of the internet (see THE INTERNET). Blogs are possibly the apogee of the internet as a way of spreading information and communication between the peoples of the world. This may suggest that the blog is a wonderful thing, a forum for debate, a place where the world comes to discuss new ideas, to learn new facts, and to become as one in cyberspace.

Fonly, as they say on the internet. Blogging is, essentially, the diary of a boring bloke in Ramsgate with too much spare time on his hands. Assembled from basic blog kits – which create the mildly appealing, if slightly minimal, local supermarket look of each and every iden-tikit blog – most weblogs are nothing more than endless lists of what someone did today. Some-times they contain lists of books and films that they saw. And – as if things weren't dazzling enough – sometimes they invite other people to contribute lists of books and films that they saw, too. Comments like '*Jarhead* – I liked this' and '*The Princess Diaries 2* – I didn't like this' build up to form a rich tapestry of criticism and debate. Wait! No, they don't.

> '**Blogging is, essentially, the diary of a boring bloke in Ramsgate with too much spare time on his hands.**'

BLOGS 2

∾

At least the boring blogs are just that – boring. They are on the Net because they are not interesting enough to be published, or not meant to be interesting enough to be published. Your bloke in Rams-gate may be vain enough to think that someone cares what he had for tea on 5 May 2006, but even he doesn't think that everyone in the world needs to know.

However, your real hardcore blogger – or 'ngmentalpatient' as they say on the Net – has no such delusions of modesty. In their eyes, the world owes them a blogging. They, you see, are not just your average nutter, because your average nutter is content to just sit next to you on the bus and explain how Atlantis is responsible for his halitosis. But your blogging nutter needs the world to know that the ant people are getting into our minds, with the help of the Jews, al Qaeda and the narrator of *Button Moon*.

He or she is an eager beaver. You can tell how eager by the special typefaces they use – really big ones, with green in them. There are lots of pictures, mostly taken from the Book of Revelation. And many of their enemies – Zionism, the Masons, the Communist Party of Great Britain, Toys 'R' Us – have thoughtfully provided logos (see LOGOS) for the blognutter to dot about their webpage like chocolate buttons on a birthday cake.

But even these are not as bad as bloggers with a cause: campaigning, single-issue bloggers who are lobbying for CHANGE via the internet and literally don't care who knows it. While their intentions are good … actually, there's no way of finding out if their intentions are good, because maybe four years ago – when they started Blogforpeace or Liberalwatch or whatever catchy, crapatronic name they sat up all night eating cane toad pie and thinking up – their blog was fairly coherent. But now, years down the line, things have got a little detailed, to say the least. 'So Governor D. Erhardt says that CO6 – or "See You're Sick", as I call it – is NOT covered by the HDB agreement? Ha!' would be a typical entry. You would have absolutely no idea what they were talking about. And nor, quite probably, would they.

CELEBRITY BLOGS
∼

Never the foaming river of anecdote, gossip and inspiration you were hoping for, celebrity blogs fall into one of the following categories:

1. **There's nothing there.** The site is still 'under construction' (see 'UNDER CONSTRUCTION') although the constructor has found time to stick up a two-year-old photo of the star. And a link to their merchandising site.

2. **There's not much there.** Just that photo, a link to the site, and a pathetic message so feeble and wet that even a fairy wouldn't leave it on its answerphone message. 'Hi, this is a Famous Person! Thanks for

taking the time to stop by! Why not check out my favourite charities? After you've visited my online store.'

3. **There's absolutely tons there.** This is because the star is a) mad, b) into a lot of causes, c) opinionated and d) thick as a wall. Fans therefore will be subjected to endless tirades about human greed (written by a millionaire who lives alone in nineteen houses made of gold), other people's vanity (this from someone with a web gallery called PHOTOS OF ME!) and the state of the world (by someone who never knows if this world is the same as the one called 'Earth' in comics).

4. **There used to be something there but now there isn't.** This is because the site was actually written by the star's 'number one fan', who got a lot of the exclusive photos, videos, quotes and free give-aways by the simple expedient of breaking into the star's house and living in their attic for three years. Sadly, the illegality of this, and the fact that the fan's weight issues meant that one day they fell through the ceiling and landed on Steven Spielberg means that the page has now been closed until the fan can get wireless installed in her prison cell (see WIRELESS).

5. There used to be a site there for the star but now it's been sold and it's a site for a brand-new girl band. *Sic transit gloria mundi*, and all that.

IPODS
∾

Hugely popular, apparently for the sole reason that they are made of white plastic. (The ones that aren't made of white plastic are popular solely because of their clever oppositional relationship to the white ones.)

But do we all have to have one? They're not that good, you know. You can't get music or photos off them unless you download a special programme. They freeze for no reason. They're worked with a stupid wheel, like they were designed by an Assyrian or something. And all the different shuffles and nanos and whatever feel like a bit of a con.

But they look nice, and that's what counts.

IPODS 2

They are admittedly a marketing triumph, even though they seem to have been invented by Isambard Kingdom Brunel. Consider the design features: instead of a funky, glow-in-the-dark, groovelicious menu, it has an incredibly dense and typefacey list of what's on it, as if written by a Dickensian clerk with an iQuill. The screen looks like the front window of a gin shop. Less tenuously, the thing is operated, like a clipper, with a huge great wheel on the front that clacked like a capstan until somebody at Apple remembered that clicking buttons had been invented.

Worse is the content. Apple make a big deal of the fact that you can 'fit' thousands of tunes in there, as though the iPod was just a sort of trunk or suitcase whose sole *raison d'être* was to be crammed with music and then, presumably, left in the attic for future generations to discover. It seems to have little to do with the fun aspect of music and more to do with a sort of Asperger's bloat.

It's just too much. Record players used to boast that they could fit six or seven singles onto their mighty spindles, and that would do your 1960s teenager nicely. Albums only contained at most 47 minutes of music, and that was fine – there is surely only so much King Crimson that even the most stoned of hippies can take.

But the iPod is a big fat whale of a thing, crammed with the hulks of a thousand musical careers, groaning with music that will almost certainly be forgotten as soon as it has been put in there. It really is the musical equivalent of those storerooms in the big museums, where every fifty years or so an assistant stumbles across an old cardboard box and says, 'Bugger me, the first nine Coldplay albums.'

How are we supposed to play these 50,000 songs? Buy a radio station and try and use them all up in a 365-day tuneathon? Invite some friends round for a dinner party and never let them leave? It's clearly impossible. The only way to do it is to hire a man and pay him to listen to your music for you.

'How are we doing today, Tomkins?'

'Halfway through the Gentle Giant, sir.'

'Good show, Tomkins.'

Mark these words: one day, someone – Apple, probably – will invent an iPod so big that they will be able to get all the recorded music in the world onto it. And when this has happened, and we have thrown away all of said music because it's recorded on out of date records, the battery on the world's biggest iPod will go flat and we won't be able to recharge it.

'SHUFFLES' AND 'NANOS'

One more thing. Having invented these enormous Hindenbergs of iPods, those good people at Apple seem secretly to realize that they have built some kind of musical black hole where your record collection will vanish forever. 'No,' they say, 'not so, we stand by our fine product, here, stick everything by the Beastie Boys in here, there's still room.' In which case, you want to ask, trying to look as lawyerly as possible, 'How come, eh, how come you have also introduced little iPods, into which you cannot cram 50,000 songs? Is it because even you find the big iPod somewhat daunting? Is it?'

'Yes,' they will say, and sneak off home to listen to a nice little Nano or Shuffle with only three songs on it, all by Girls Aloud and quite pleasant for all that.

TEXT MESSAGING

Apparently it's not as common in America. Which probably means they have more bees, because, as surely we all know, bees are confused by the magic wireless rays of mobile phones and get lost. It's all rather sad, but just one example of the many flaws of text messaging.

Text messaging began innocuously enough. It was, in many ways, the slightly more advanced descendant of the pager. Remember them? You would phone up a woman and tell them something, like, 'Billy, come home, for it's tea time,' or, 'Doctor Lanyard, everyone keeps falling over,' and Billy or Doctor Lanyard would get a sudden buzzing in their pager, then look at the pager. This would display your message in enormous greeny-grey capitals and so they would phone you back.

This system had the great advantage that, to call someone back, you had to get to a phone. And, thus so doing, have a conversation, and get all the talking-about-the problem gubbins out of the way. Once done with the phone conversation, Billy or Doctor Lanyard could get back to whatever it was they were doing earlier.

Not so with text messaging, or 'texting', as it has become known in this crazy, abbreviation-obsessed world. Texting is not text messaging, because it's no longer about sending a message. A message is TWO PINTS PLEASE, MILKMAN or HELP, I AM ON A DESERT ISLAND. A text message is nothing more or less than the warning shot before a conversation. If you receive a text – something like 'Hi how are u' – you are tricked, like someone forced to play chess, into a round of pushbutton chatter. You are compelled to reply: 'I am fine TY how u?' (notice how much finer your grammar is). And then you've had it. Locked – headlocked – in a conversation that ten seconds ago you didn't even know you were going to have.

TEXT MESSAGING 2

~

Text messaging is a subtle thing, because, like a really tiny nuclear bomb, it harms nobody but you. Having a conversation on a mobile phone (see MOBILE PHONES) can get you into trouble, as people start shushing you and all that. But the only sign that you are texting is the frantic click-click of your fingers on the too-small keyboard and the deepening frown on your forehead.

You are infinitely traceable, too. There's no pretending that you've 'got no signal'. Texts are able to get through on the tiniest amount of signal, and will follow you like heat-seeking missiles. And so you are expected to reply. And once again, there you are.

There is, of course, nothing intrinsically wrong with being trace-able, or with having extremely shorthandy conversations with your friends and loved ones. It's just that it's extremely difficult. And text messages from other people always have this in common: they are couched in the form of a simple, easy-to-type question, but always require a complex answer that needs every ounce of your linguistic skills.

For example, a simple text like, 'Did it go OK at doctor?' can't be left hanging with a basic 'Yes'. You have to text in, 'Pretty good, it seems I am entirely free of pleurisy.' Neither do these words ever turn up on predictive texting (see PREDICTIVE TEXTING) – although it is a fair bet that, if you are trying to write a different message, the phone will seize on this new word 'pleurisy' and use it instead of 'please' or 'Plumstead'.

And so it goes on. You never get a text saying, 'Wot did u eat 4 lunch' when you've just had a pot pie. No, you will find yourself sitting there, as the waiter hovers with the bill, trying to key in the words, '*tagliatelle alla matriciana*' and '*zuppa pavese con parmigiano*'. In the end you give up and just put 'Chips'.

And why is it that the only message you never seem to get via text is 'Call me'? Possibly because if, after you've virtually broken every bone in your hand trying to text someone a vaguely complicated message, you've actually gone and phoned them, you always get put straight through to voicemail.

PREDICTIVE TEXTING
∾

Like nuclear power, tennis and Esperanto, predictive texting was probably invented with the best motives in mind. It came along, you may recall, at a time when text messaging was slow and painful. Originally, phone keypads were designed to work a bit like, well, like phone keypads, with all those ABCs and DEFs clustered over the actual numbers, and a bit like a typewriter. So if you wanted – don't worry, this will be over soon – if you wanted to write the word POTATO, you'd hover over the keypad jabbing letters one by one until finally you got the word POTABO.

Predictive texting made it its life's message to change all that. It was determined that no longer would we have to jab and stab to create words. After all, computers could guess what we were about to write, and, with simple instant spellchecking programmes, could correct our errors too. So why not apply the same process to mobile phones?

Because, it turns out, mobile phones are to computers what crudely made tiny clay ponies are to Arab stallions. Bluntly speaking, mobile phones are not very bright. (If they were very bright, they'd be breathing germs into us, and not the other way round.) They're just not up to the job of predicting what we're going to say next.

And why should they be? Our own wives and loved ones can't do it either. If you don't expect your best friend to guess what noun is coming when you say, 'I think I'm going to …' and he doesn't know whether to shout, 'Marry Claire! Hurray!' or 'Throw up everywhere! Quick, let me get a bucket', then we cannot expect a mobile phone that hardly even knows us to do better.

The poor things get it wrong time after time. They can't tell 'lettuce' from 'Leicester'. They don't know 'Auntie Mary' from 'anger management'. And it's not just the long words, either. Many phones have the extraordinary habit of totally losing their cool and turning very simple words like 'don't' into 'foot'.

Weirdly, though, in all this chaos, phones have one strangely prissy quality. Like the Queen and unlike parrots, mobile phones with predictive texting hardly ever swear. But then that, one supposes, is your job.

MOBILE PHONES
~

There is no doubt that – as with penicillin, votes for women and the *Police Academy* movies – mobile phones have completely and utterly transformed our world.

It will do us no harm to go back in time and revisit an era before mobile phones were common. Was it only less than twenty years ago? It must be, because in the 1980s any mobile phones you saw were just one step up the evolutionary ladder from either walkie-talkies or those weird 'field phones' they had in war films, where one soldier carried the bloody thing and the other got to hold the handset and crank a little turny thing.

They were, as every comedian and *I Love the Eighties* talking head has noticed since, absolutely enormous. And not very mobile, either. They had two problems: one was the size, making anyone rich enough to use one look like they were listening very closely to a robot's foot. And the other was the battery capacity. Each phone had to be charged up, roughly every seven seconds, by one of the boxes they used to trap ghosts in from the movie *Ghostbusters*.

They were rubbish and, some say, we should have taken advantage of their weakness and killed them then. But we didn't and mobile phones swiftly evolved. Soon they were small, and efficient, and only needed charging once a day (which in some ways makes them worryingly superior to their human 'masters'). And then they became omnipresent. Super omnipresent. Suddenly it seemed that everyone in the world had one, and if they didn't they had a friend with two, which made up for it.

And now they rule the world, controlling us with their microwave rays and making us spend hundreds of pounds on upgrades and SIM cards and SMSes, whatever they are. We should have acted when we had the chance.

MOBILE PHONES 2

∿

Less dramatically, one of the vexing things about mobile phones is not that they are everywhere (although that is quite vexing) but that they enable you to be tracked down wherever you are. That's *wherever* you are, any time, any place. Even, these days, in the middle of the Gobi Desert. ('Hi, I'm on the Przewalski horse, yeah, I'll be home soon.') In space. ('I told you not to call me when I'm fixing the solar – damn! There goes another one!') At the bottom of the sea. ('No, it must be your end. I can hear you fine.')

Surely this must be a good thing? Surely it must be right and decent that we can be contacted wherever we go (except in a horror or detective film, in which mobile phones never ever work)? Not so. Back in

PORTABLE D[...]

The ability to operate [...]
radiotelephone from a [...]
telephone system has [...]
sible, but now Pye [...]
ability to dial from a [...]
telephone (no need for s[...]
if it were an ordinary [...]
phone.

'Not very mobile.'

the day, if you were out, you were out. People had to phone the place you said you might be, or just leave it. This gave us all a possibly illusory but still reassuring sense of freedom. You're out on your own, and nobody can bother you until you choose to let them. That way, a simple visit to Fine Fare was as good as a hike across the Yorkshire Moors. A visit to the dentist was made almost pleasurable by the knowledge that, for all the world knew, you were doing an Agatha Christie and spending a month in a hotel, wondering who the hell you were and why you were wearing that ridiculous hat.

But now? People can find you at any time. The art of honest skiving has been wiped out at a stroke. You can't just nip behind a wall, like a tramp in a 1930s comic being pursued by coppers, and never be seen again. You are on the world's radar and you can be found at any minute.

And it's no good turning the bloody thing off or pretending that some sinister men took it from you. Your boss or your loved ones will instinctively know that you turned it off, just to avoid them. And then a big van will come and take you away and put you in a special room. And just as you sigh and relax for the first time, your mobile phone rings.

MOBILE PHONES 3
〜

Not to go on about this, but they're not even phones any more. Again, what happened to the world we used to have? We used not to feel the need to go everywhere with a phone, a camera, a video camera, a notebook, a set of tiny computer games, an MP3 player (see MP3s), the internet and the name and address of everyone we've ever met. But that's exactly what we do with a mobile phone.

We have become unwitting Boy Scouts of the twenty-first century, prepared for every eventuality with our Swiss Army phones. We may not be able to take stones out of horses' hooves with our phones, but we don't need to. If we do see a horse, we can just take its photograph. Which we can then text to all our friends, with the caption, 'Look! A horse.' Twenty years ago not only would you not have had a camera with you, but also you wouldn't have wanted to take a picture of a horse, and you'd have been very unlikely to have sent a picture of a horse to your friends. Because the next time they saw you, they'd have said, 'Hey, why'd you send me a picture of a horse?'

And you wouldn't have had a proper answer.

COMPACT DISCS
∾

There's nothing sadder than the future after it's been sacked. CDs were the emperors of sound technology back in their day. Men in suits almost as shiny as the compact discs they were demonstrating would carefully slide the tray into the little slot, press a button and then ooh! and ahh! Music would come out. Shiny, bright, clean music. The fact that the music was a bit too shiny and bright and clean didn't matter. Nor did the fact that there was no bass to speak of. People who lived in quickly built flats in dockland developments didn't want bass. Their walls might collapse.

Like that other shiny, clean and bright 80s thing, Tears For Fears, CDs ran the world. Like the Soviet Union, they were apparently indestructible. You could put jam on them and they'd still play, although it was never satisfactorily explained why anybody would want to put jam on a CD, and in fact it wasn't true. If you put jam on a CD, it wouldn't work any more. Nor were they, as was claimed, scratchproof.

And so, after fifteen years of power, the CD – tinny, scratched, covered in jam and with a sleeve that only ants could read – ceded its dominance to the MP3 file (see MP3s).

MP3s
∾

The latest best thing in the history of communications, MP3s do have many advantages. They are, if you're still struggling with sheet music as a concept, little computer thingies which are the size of an ant's thumb, and which are somehow full of music. Thanks to the miracle of broadband, they can be downloaded onto your computer and – WAKE UP! – and you can listen to extraordinary quantities of music on a machine the size of a large, flat notebook. Apparently this is brilliant.

It's hard to see why, though. As any technogeek will tell you, MP3s don't actually sound that brilliant. Audio-wise, they're better than a cassette (see CASSETTES) and worse than a CD (see COMPACT DISCS) which, given that CDs are apparently worse than vinyl (see VINYL), suggests that things aren't as good as they might be (see CROSS-REFERENCES, EXCESS OF).

Ah, say people who like to say 'Ah', but these are early days, and the audio quality will surely improve, and what sounds right now like Jim Morrison singing into his fist under a pile of canvas will one day sound like Jim Morrison riding a lovely golden surfboard around a room full of cymbals. So that's all right then.

MP3s 2
~

Except it isn't all right. The other thing about the MP3 is, where other music carriers (see ... oh all right) are massive great steak and kidney pies of tunes and tracks, stuffed with as much music as possible, the MP3 is more of an individual fruit pie, small and solitudinous. Vinyl records and CDs and so forth were big feasts of music, with singles and album tracks and the ballad and the filler track and the one by the drummer all cheek by jowl. It made for a Proper Listening Experience.

MP3s, however, come One Tune at a Time. They are like singles, except often not as good. But the people who are selling us MP3s wish to emphasize their singularity. They point out that, by buying songs in ones, you are missing out on the duff stuff. You can make your own playlist! And call it something really imaginative like, 'Eighties on the Go', or, 'I Only Know Three Heavy Metal Songs'.

But the thing about the ballad and the one by the drummer, and even the filler track, is that they did sound good in context. More than the sum of their parts, they added up to something – like *Revolver*, or *Nevermind*, or *Here Come the Wurzels*.

Buying MP3s is like buying bits of a jigsaw, or a sandwich, or a book, in instalments. It's somewhat unsatisfying (and muffled). And you can't leave MP3s lying around your flat to impress visitors, either.

SMART CARS
∽

They look like kettles. What's smart about that?

LAPTOPS
∽

Everyone's got one these days. You can't get on a train or go into a Starbucks (see PEOPLE WHO HAVE MEETINGS IN STAR-BUCKS) without seeing some gimpaloid with a laptop on his perspiring thighs, tapping away like a bad Scrabbler with a rotten hand. And what is this person doing? Is he creating a work of art so great that it must needs be chiselled into a document straightaway? Has he found the cure for the common cold? No. He is killing time until his friend arrives by pretending to be an important business boy. Because there can be no work so essential that it has to be done in public. Because a train compartment or a seat in a coffee house are not offices. Because sitting there with a laptop has become the modern equivalent of getting on a train and phoning up everyone and telling them you're on the train. 'Hi! I've got wireless!' NOBODY CARES.

'There can be no work so essential that it has to be done in public.'

SELF CHECK-OUT

∿

Or whatever it's called. That thing where you're in the supermarket and instead of going to the check-out and having a girl do the beep beep bit with your stuff, you do it yourself. The idea is either to keep queues down or to get rid of loads of burdensome, minimum-wage-earning supermarket staff.

Either way, it doesn't bloody work. For a kick off, you still have to queue because the pillock in front of you can't work the machine and so a massive queue forms behind him. And then, after a lot of searching, he finds and presses the I AM RUBBISH button, which summons over a man in a shirt and tie who does know how it works. They might as well keep all the staff on, as they are the only ones who know how the bastard machine works.

Not only that, but when it finally is your turn, and you make your way to the front, full of contempt and derision for the fool who couldn't work the scanner, you discover that in fact you can't work the scanner either. You repeatedly wave the bar code over the glass thing and it fails to beep in a reassuring way.

Eventually, you manage it, and reach for the last item in your basket. It is a strange-looking vegetable, something your partner requested as part of the ingredients for dinner, and it is also something you've never heard of. Nor, it seems, has the scanner. There is no bar code, and the handy table of Individual Vegetables nearby doesn't list it.

In the end, as the queue behind you grows tetchier, you decide that it looks a bit like a courgette, so you press COURGETTE and pay. And as you leave, you are arrested for stealing a Prussian fennel stalk, and go to jail for the rest of your life.

SELF CHECK-IN

∿

As if air travel wasn't difficult enough. These days airports have got so lazy that they don't even want to check you in any more. This would be fine – there are only so many bad-tempered men and women in pretend Thunderbirds outfits that one should meet in a lifetime. However, there is nothing weirder than trying to arrange your own flight details through a machine that looks as though it would have difficulty issuing a single to Bond Street, let alone enabling you to wing your way across the azure skies.

It has all the bad qualities of a real check-in with real people – it asks you a lot of dim questions about who packed your bag and so forth, and it takes all day about it – but unlike a real check-in, it keeps getting stuck and telling you to key in things that make no sense to you, like your AIRLINE PIN or your SPECIAL TRAVELLER CODE.

The only good thing about the self check-in machine is that at least when it gives you a seat in the very last row of economy, when you'd asked for a nice aisle seat because of your bad back, it doesn't laugh quietly under its breath. But they're working on that.

THE INTERNET

There's a period in the history of science fiction (see SCIENCE FICTION) known as the Gernsback era, probably. Named after the founder of the early SF magazine *Amazing Stories* or something, the Gernsback era refers to that lovely time when writers of that sort of stuff imagined a world where giant twenty-propellered airships played host to parties where space jazz bands made music for silver-suited astrofolk to dance to as they pointed at the shiny silver rocket-ships heading for chrome-lined colonies on Mars.

Of course, this never happened – NO! REALLY?! – and millions of baby boomers pretended to get upset about it and a lot of this happened:

SECOND-RATE STAND-UP COMEDIAN:
I thought we were supposed to have food pills in the future? And, er …

AUDIENCE:
Jetpacks!

And much the same thing happened, in real life, with the internet. (Remember when it was the World Wide Web? What a great, noble, clunky, unusable name that was. When it was 'shortened' to www, it become one of the few instances of an abbreviation that was actually harder to say than the original phrase.)

The internet began in an exciting, sinister way. Invented – apparently – by your classic nice British scientist, as he absent-mindedly smoked a chrome space pipe on his way home from the jetpack shop, it was designed for a Military Purpose. The idea was, broadly and vaguely, to design a communications system that would survive a nuclear war. How this would have worked has never been satisfactorily explained. Logically, they should have trained cockroaches to carry messages. But they didn't.

And as time went on, slowly the internet evolved, until even the aristocracy could use it. Nowadays hundreds, maybe even thousands, of people go online every day, to look up useful information, chat with old friends, and generally improve the quality of life on earth. Oh hang on – and look at pornography, and send spam (see SPAM) and exchange unfunny mpegs of self-abusing monkeys, and bid their life savings on auction sites (see INTERNET AUCTION SITES).

In short, the internet has been a complete waste of time. Not only has it become a way for every freak, nutter and criminal on the planet to get into your house and hassle you, but it also uses vast and vaster amounts of power, resources and that fossil-fuel stuff to run itself. The horrible thing about the collapse of civilization is that T.S. Eliot was right, even though he wrote *Cats*: the world will end, not with the bang of a million nuclear missiles, but with the whimper of the internet dying as the last of the world's resources is used up by an office worker in Hull sending the man in the next cubicle a picture of a naked lady.

SPAM
∾

Not the meat, no, that's quite nice, especially as fritters. This is internet spam, and spam's real claim to fame is that it is the one thing in the world that nobody likes. Except, obviously, the people who write it, and they probably don't like receiving other people's spam. But that might not be the case, either. Spam is so weird that it fits into no known category of annoyance.

Before spam, we had junk mail – actual pieces of paper in actual envelopes posted through your actual letterbox. Junk mail was horrible, but at least it made sense. Its lies – YOU HAVE WON A YACHT, OR A HOUSE, OR A PEN! SEND ALL YOUR MONEY TO SOME CRIMINALS, TODAY! – were somehow coherent, and seemed to have been written by one of the people of earth. Similarly, cold-calling – 'Hello, is that Mr Jones? Oh, am I speaking to the lady of the house? Good, buy some central heating or your head will fall off' – had some relation to human crime as we knew it.

But spam is just astonishingly weird. It is, admittedly, designed with three purposes in mind:

1. To get you to send money.
2. To get you to reply and confirm your internet existence.
3. To get round all the various security protocols that allegedly exist out there.

And it is this third point – getting round things – that gives spam its peculiarness. Because spam, or spams, or spamming, or whatever it is, or are, has developed into a strange culture of its own. Certain things, phrases and ideas occur again and again. It looks like there are rules in the world of spam (see THE RULES OF SPAM).

THE RULES OF SPAM
✑

1. To alert people to the possibility that this email is fake, spell random words wrong: 'Wellcome! How are yau? Let's meat up!' And so forth.

2. To further alert the reader (and, if we're being honest, to get round security and because we haven't got a pukka email address), have a return email address that sounds almost right, but isn't, like 'PayPal.co.crimeylandnet'.

3. For the purposes of reassuring the easily fooled recipient, make sure that your email doesn't just say, 'We are a bunch of crooks, send all your bank details now.' Be subtle. Pretend you are a bank or something and you've just sort of forgotten their security details and would they mind awfully emailing them back to you?

4. To ensnare the greedy internet user – the one who before they discovered email was always buying the Brooklyn Bridge half-price and so forth – offer them a fantastic business opportunity that only they have been picked for.

This opportunity must consist solely of a special kind of letter, which goes a bit like this:

Hello good sir and woman! I am the legal and right representative of the formal government in exile of Madeupland and have been authorized to write you this email by His Royal Emince Mrs Alan Pankhurst, OBE. Her Serenity advises me to let you know that she plans to return to power in a really soon time. But to do that such, she needs of a lot of money. You have been chosen for your honesty face at random from a special list.

If you would please send us either a Czech or a moneyed order to PayPal.co.crimeylandnet, for the somme of fifteen millions of your pounds in dollars and euros, we will guarantee that not will you receive in full all of some of that of none of that money back, but you will be thanked with a medallion by our government when we are return to power. Hurray for that and send us the money now. We are waiting, hurry up.

It is believed that many of these letters are fake.

5. When offering products that promote sexual vigour, however, there are two options: a) be as blunt and forward in your language as possible, to draw in people who aren't quite sure what it is exactly that Viagra does, or b) offer a message of such powerful reassurance that nobody can resist, like, 'She will love you like no other man' or 'You will get a big willy'.

6. Quote bits of books at random in a really frightening way. 'And his hands moved towards the older pendulum.' 'Or were they shoes, it was always hard to tell.' This rarely makes anyone want to reply to your emails, but it does freak the crap out of people.

7. Be absolutely, totally, completely incomprehensible. 'Seven yes is days of our spotulism.' 'Millways to free down upwards any breakwater! Half pretend.' This may make people reply to your emails in the mistaken belief that you are trying to cross over from the spirit world, via email.

8. Just to be really vexing, use a Christian name like 'John' or 'Debbie' because the chances are quite high that many of the people you are spamming actually know a John or Debbie and will unthinkingly open an email from them, only to find that Debbie thinks their winkle is too small and John would like to smarket down repeat the gasjumpet yes to hufferly.

9. Finally, take comfort in the fact that so many people are on the lookout for spam that they routinely delete anything that looks a bit like spam, which, given that spam looks a little bit like everything else, means that most of us are happily deleting emails from real people every day, and wondering why we don't have any friends any more.

10. Remember – anyone foolish enough to fall for your illegal evil criminal vile trick is a sucker and so it's their fault. Ha ha ha!

POP UPS
∾

Those things that just, well, pop up when you are trying to read your emails. Does anyone in the world ever think, 'Oh good, an unfunny graphic with three gurning bozos in it and a crappy slogan – I'd much rather have this filling up my entire screen than the email I have been trying to write for the last twenty-five minutes.'

In an ideal world, the people who come up with pop ups should, when walking to work, have people jump in front of them with huge bits of cardboard while shouting inane advertising slogans. It's the only language they understand.

CHAT ROOMS
❧

They're not rooms. This may sound like pedantry, but calling chat rooms 'rooms' makes them sound like shelters, cozy havens for pals to get together and, well, 'chat'. And thank God, too. Imagine being locked in a room, in the dark, with a bunch of – let's be honest here – weirdos. Because frankly nobody normal ever uses a chat room. 'Oh, I'd really like to meet a bunch of strangers who are too weird to use their own names. Perhaps they'll be borderline illiterate, too!'

There's another thing about chat rooms. They're not places where you chat, either. A chat is a relaxed, casual conversation, a pleasant exchange of news and views between two or more friends. What it is not is this:

CHICKEN645: u there?
DARTHTAYLOR: what I was saying was
DARTHTAYLOR: i liked the first film but
MISSISKIPPERS: hello i am sexy
DARTHTAYLOR: i think the new ones
333BILBO: did anyone see hollyoaks
CHICKEN645: u there?
DARTHTAYLOR: that was my mobile sorry
333BILBO: i didn't tape it
MISSISKIPPERS: i would like to meet
333BILBO: get off this page u porno
DARTHTAYLOR: what I was saying was
333BILBO: so has anyone got a video
333BILBO: of hollyoaks
CHICKEN645: u there?

I.e. the incoherent babbling of six or twenty people, all using false names and none of whom has the slightest interest in what the others are saying. Chat rooms are horrible places, almost certainly identical to that bit in the Bible where everyone who lived in the Tower of Babel was made to speak in different languages for some God-related reason.

CHAT ROOMS 2
∽

A nd even if you did want to join in a 'chat', the whole business is a special sort of nightmare. For a start, as every second-rate stand-up knows, most of the people in chat rooms are pretending to be someone else:

SECOND-RATE STAND-UP COMEDIAN:
And when I met her, she wasn't a twenty-one-year-old pole dancer – she was a twenty-one-stone lorry driver!

AUDIENCE:
Oh, we have so heard that one before.

And even if they're not, then they do have one thing in common. They're really dull. Really, really dull. anthillmob91 has only one topic, namely her cat. CudlyDudly just wants to talk about his divorce. And Elephantmanchester is an American online prankster, pretending to be a pervert to get filler for his website.

It wouldn't be so bad (all right, it would be so bad, but it would be a different so bad) if all this crap and toss took up only a few seconds of your time. But it doesn't. It takes ages. You can't follow a conversation because every time you write something down, five hundred other people who are Really Not Listening leap in and write a load of toot about their own boring stupid misspelled illiterate lives.

'UNDER CONSTRUCTION'
∽

A slightly manly phrase in the circumstances, 'under construction' suggests a degree of determined sweatiness in a major cause. Men in big plastic hats building things. Huge hotels and cathedrals on the way to dominating skylines. Big yellow metal machines doing digging and creating dust. That sort of thing.

What it does not, or rather ought not, bring to mind, is some nerdoid in his bedroom who can't be bothered to make a proper website but still wants us all to visit it, so he puts up a sign saying 'Under Construction' to make us think that he is toiling under massive pressure to bring the world a skyscraper of a website. When really he's sitting on his bed playing Tomb Raider in his underwear.

WIRELESS
❧

It's funny how certain words survive. When the word 'wireless' first came along, it meant a radio, generally one shaped like a loaf of bread with a dial on it covered in words like 'Hilversum'. Now it means an internet system that can be used in lots of different rooms and you can, in fact, if you have a laptop, carry it from room to room like a baby that won't go to sleep.

The first thing about this is what's so good about this? Why can't we sit still? 'I'm bored reading my emails in the front room, I think I'll go and see if they're more interesting in that little room we keep the old ironing board in.'

We don't ever feel the urge to move the bath to the dining room, or have a toilet fitted in the living room, so why is the internet such a moveable feast? Do we worry that it'll get piles if it stays in the same place?

The answer, ironically, is that we have to keep moving it round because the signal is weak. Like someone with an old-school mobile (see MOBILE PHONES), we go from room to room, waving the laptop up and down a bit and turning, hoping vainly to be able to read that email that is probably spam but might actually be from Beyoncé. Still, it's the only exercise we get these days.

CD ROMS
~

These promise the earth, but always turn out to contain the following:

1. A computer programme that doesn't work on your computer.
2. Some of a new computer game, but not enough to actually play.
3. A pop video by someone you hate.
4. A recipe by someone you hate.
5. Plans of the secret tunnels under the Louvre that will enable you to steal the Mona Lisa. Unfortunately, you can't access this because it's an 'Easter Egg' and you're not quite sure how they work.

SECOND LIFE
~

Another troubling symptom of modern life. Science-fiction writers (see SCIENCE FICTION) have long predicted that, one day, mankind will flee its fleshy prison and the turmoils of the real world and 'upload' itself into 'cyberspace'. True, science-fiction writers have predicted all sorts of nonsense over the years, from men in the Moon to shoes that can argue, but in this case they're almost right.

Because, while people are as yet unable to live in cyberspace – possibly because there's no such flaming thing as cyberspace – they have begun to build sad, slightly gay (see 'GAY') lives for themselves on this Second Life thing.

Second Life is essentially a cross between an insanely dull computer game or a badly drawn cartoon version of *Emmerdale*. It's a 'virtual (see 'VIRTUAL') world' where you take on an identity, get a badly drawn cartoon and go round doing stuff that you couldn't do in real life, like fly, or be interesting.

The name is bad enough. The phrase 'Second Life' implies that the user already has a First Life. Given that the user is an internet nerd who has enough spare time to pretend to be a badly drawn cartoon fox who lives in a laptop, this seems unlikely.

Then there's the whole fantasy element. This is meant to be a real world, but everyone is about seven feet tall, has names like Frummers Impetigo, flies around everywhere, and looks like one of two things: Sonic the Hedgehog or Lara Croft.

As the world slips into all kinds of terrible trouble, it's understandable that people might want to escape. But surely all this scientific knowhow and imagination might be put to better use? Like, say, bringing an end to global warming. Or building a huge spaceship and colonizing other, weaker planets. Either way, the sooner they find a way to actually 'upload' all these people into cyberspace, the better.

WEBCAMS
~

Webcams have had a very weird life, considering. They are, technically, cameras, but they don't seem to bear any similarity to cameras in any way other than the bit about having a lens and showing images.

It's like this. In the Victorian era, when things were changing rapidly, and the world looked set to be swamped entirely by top hats and steam trains, somebody didn't sit down and think, Blimey, painting all these new inventions is going to take years. I think I'd better invent the camera. Because the idea behind the camera is very simple. Somebody saw something interesting, like a particularly big top hat or shiny steamboat, and what they actually thought was, Oh, that's interesting, I'd like a record of that. And so they fiddled about with plates and magnesium and so forth and it was all flash bang wallop – what a picture what a photograph (to quote Henri Cartier-Bresson). Cameras were invented so that we could have a look at that interesting thing.

And the same thing happened with film cameras. 'Wow! That's really exciting! We need to get that down for posterity!' And the same with television cameras, only here the law of diminishing returns kicks in. After all, there's a big difference, 'interesting'-wise, between, say, *Gone with the Wind* and *Home and Away*. But cameras continued to be useful and fun, especially CCTV cameras (see CCTV). Until the invention of the webcam, that is.

Webcams are one of the worst and most annoyingly stupid ideas in the history of otioseness. They are, in case you were out during the invention of computers, cameras that connect to the internet. And so, in theory, you can watch anything, anywhere in the world, at any time, on a webcam.

You'd think that idea would inspire millions to leap into action, wouldn't you? You'd think that everywhere that something thrilling was happening, there'd be a webcam. In fact, you'd imagine that the mere presence of a webcam would be an indicator to the world that something pretty exciting was going on, would you not? Well (as you may have guessed by the petulant sarcasm of the last few sentences), you'd be wrong.

Webcams were apparently invented by someone who thought, What the world needs now is the ability to look at an industrial estate on the Wirral. That's 'look at an industrial estate on The Wirral' twenty-four hours a day, seven days a week. And what's happened on this industrial estate? Is it being occupied by a blue viral moss creature from another world? Are thousands of linnets forming an avian pyramid? Has David Bowie appeared, naked save for a cocked hat, in the middle of the car park? None of these things. It's just an industrial estate. Sometimes a car comes. Sometimes a car doesn't. NOTHING HAPPENS.

And nothing also happens in lots of other places around the world. A car park in Reno. A breakwater in Porchester Regis. A tree in Who Gives a Toss. And so on. It's incredibly boring and an astonishing waste of technology, effort and resources. It's not funny or ironic, either. It's just rubbish.

WEBCAMS 2
∾

Of course, there are webcams that don't just look at empty spaces. Not counting the rude kind, where people pay hundreds of quid to look at a naked woman in her bedroom doing peculiar things (because any perv with a stepladder can get that for free), there is one particularly dull kind of webcam – the Nerdcam.

It's probably not called that. But it should be. Around the world there are thousands of nerds whose sole joy it is to stick a camera on top of their bedroom door, or worse, their head, and let the world see their drab, dull, deadly doings.

People – well, other nerds – tune in to see this horror. They watch as the nerd with the camera goes online, and talks to some other nerds. They look as the nerd puts on his helmet Nerdcam and goes for a walk to the local internet café, and talks to some more other nerds. And then he goes home, turns out the lights and goes to bed. Leaving the Nerdcam on, so we can watch him sleep.

VIDEOPHONES
⌇

We are all now familiar with the concept that we never got the future we were expecting. People have written excellent books about what happened to jetpacks and underwater cities and food pills, but the one that seemed to be rammed down our throats every week by the primitive 1970s media (especially *Tomorrow's World*, which must surely hold the title of Least Accurate Science Programme of All Time) was the videophone.

Remember when we were all going to have videophones? A normal phone, except it was attached to either a tiny little screen in the base or, if you had the deluxe version, an absolutely massive wall-crippling screen that took up half the house. Making a videophone call would be exactly like making a normal one, except you could see the other person talking to you. It was therefore exciting, even if it didn't take account of the fact that, in most people's houses, the videophone would probably ring when the family had sat down to have their food pills.

Videophones, like webcams (see WEBCAMS), were meant to be exciting. It was all going to be, 'Hi, I'm calling from Mars!' and, 'Look everyone! Moon rocks!' But it didn't turn out that way. Because now, in a way, we have videophones on our computers. Those little cameras on top of the computer that with various modern computer programmes and little microphones we can use to chat to each other across the wifi ether. And do we chat about moon rocks and life on

Mars? No, of course we don't. We say things like, 'Hi, I'm in Rhyl!' and 'Look at my bedroom! Don't I have a lot of *Star Wars* posters?'

VIDEO-CONFERENCING

The worst thing ever. Taking as our starting point the idea that there is nothing worse than a business meeting for sheer, undiluted, pointless, dull, boring, dull and boring WHAT FOR?-ness, then surely the concept of a video-conference must be all that only cubed. The idea, like the person who thought of it, is simple. When you have a meeting and one of the terribly important suits (who you want to be there so she or he can be as bored as you are) can't make it because they're in Manchester, what you do is get them into a room in Manchester, set up a couple of cameras and screens and hey detesto! You're video-conferencing! It's great! It's like a real meeting except one of you is on a tiny screen by the coffee-maker and everything they say comes out of their mouths ten seconds after they've said it. Like someone translating for a lip-reader. And they're in a boardroom on their own and they're happy because they get to eat all the biscuits, but nobody else is because video-conferencing just adds a special new extra layer of boringness to a meeting.

The only good thing about video-conferencing is that you can go behind the TV screen when the person on it is talking and make faces. Which hardly justifies your company spending eight million quid on a video-conferencing system. But almost does.

VIRTUAL ENCYCLOPAEDIAS

It's hard to believe now but, back in the day, encyclopaedias were so common that they had their own salesmen. No, let's be even more specific about this. Back in the day, encyclopaedia salesmen were so common that there were jokes about them. Imagine – there once was a world where great big books with lots of entries about all the stuff that there is were actually enormously popular. And none of these books were written by FILL IN NAME OF ENORMOUSLY

POPULAR AUTHOR WHO NEVER GETS GOOD REVIEWS HERE. You know, that guy.

Times, as you may have noticed simply by staring out of the window at the mannequin across the road in the shop display whose clothes keep whizzing on and off, are changing (so much so that the traditional 'a-' which always accompanied the word 'changing' has been dropped). Very few people nowadays buy actual encyclopaedias, apart from maybe wizards and people in old sitcoms who need to make one leg of a table somewhat higher. These days, we don't need actual encyclopaedias because we have got virtual ones (see 'VIRTUAL').

The virtual encyclopaedia is not like a regular, made-of-trees-and-ink encyclopaedia. Those were written by eighty old men in a room that smelt of bones over a very long period of time and you had to be the world's oldest expert on something that began with D to even think about writing 300 words on dropsy, or desks, or DMC, Run. And to get that job, you had to have been vetted by someone like Isaac Newton or Albert Einstein, and even then you weren't allowed to write the introduction, which was always so bizarre and incomprehensible that it was probably a secret message to Stalin.

But the internet is different. Like a jellyfish that wants to be your friend but is never in when you call, the internet spreads promiscuously and formlessly over the globe, inviting all and sundry to participate in its adventures. And so it is with internet encyclopaedias. They are not the product of the ripest fruits of Academe. They are instead the product of some very odd people indeed. Like geeks, only geekier. Like nerds, only nerdier. Like, in some ways, professors, only without qualifications forged in the hot smithies of university.

So some virtual encyclopaedias are great. Even the ones that aren't often have very splendid entries. But there's always a risk with your virtual encyclopaedia. For every beautifully researched article that goes like this:

VAN MARKUS, EHRICH (1827–1901)
The first Emeritus Professor of Cosmology (see Baklava, Cosmology And The Prussians) in the contemporary sense of the

word, Van Markus was also the first person to explain clearly the difference between astrology and astronomy (cf: Claymore, *Astronomers are the Ones with Telescopes*) and usher in the modern era of scientific stellar exploration.

there are about 47 million that go like this:

VAN MARKUS (ROCK group, LOS ANGELES, 1990 or something)
Van Markus are the best band in the world really they are. Their first album, Van Markus II, is probably the best altho it's hard to say because a) the third one is pretty good and b) I don't really have all the other ones.

Also there is apparently this whole business with the virtual encyclopaedia known as 'deliberately making things up'. So an entry about, say, Abba will be deliberately disrupted by some malicious person writing an entry on the lines of 'Abba were actually lizards and split up when their tails fell off'. Which you rarely get with a proper encyclopaedia. Well, fairly rarely …

SHAKESPEARE, WILLIAM (1564–1616)
Author of arguably the most significant canon of plays in the history of English, if not world, drama. Authorship of Shakespeare's plays is sometimes attributed to Francis Bacon (1561–1626). And Bagpuss (February 1974–May 1974). You know, the big fluffy cat.

'VIRTUAL'
◦

'Virtual' in the modern sense doesn't mean something like 'almost', as in 'I was virtually sober when I stole that car, your honour'. It means … well, no one really knows what it means – no one who's ever had a relationship or any friends, anyway – but it seems to mean 'on the internet'. Thus, we get 'virtual encyclopaedia', which means 'a jumble of ill-informed nonsense on the internet (see VIRTUAL ENCYCLOPAEDIAS), 'virtual sex', which means 'playing with yourself on the internet', and 'virtual reality', which means 'just really bad computer graphics'.

CCTV
∾

The only fun in town. CCTV was apparently invented to provide security in our teeming plazas and busy shopping malls. And of course it has been a roaring success. With police officers now able to recognize known villains from tiny, blurry, pixellated images, if the villains have taken their balaclavas off, crime is at an all-time low and hardly anyone gets robbed, beaten up or stabbed any more.

Well, perhaps that's not entirely true. In actual fact, CCTV is completely bloody useless, an infringement of our civil liberties that provides about as much security as a suit of armour made from Wet Wipes. It does, however, have one advantage over ID cards (see ID CARDS). It's great for providing footage for TV-clip shows. The police may never catch the fat dude who robbed a convenience store in Idaho and then had his trousers fall down, but at least his comedy antics provided up to 30 seconds of cheap entertainment on *Smile! You're a Crap Robber!*

COKE ZERO™
∾

How come it's not Diet Coke? Is it for people who are so fat from drinking regular (i.e. sugar-sodden) Coke that they can no longer look at the word 'diet' without feeling bad? Is Coke Zero then for people who are actually TOO FAT TO DIET?

ROBOTS
∿

Over the last hundred or so years, robots have been arguably the coolest of man's foes (although that's not saying much, as some of man's other foes are cockroaches, pigeons and premature baldness). Designed allegedly to look like us – although more of that in a second – so that we will be reassured by their humanly presence, in fact robots scare the knickers off us with their immobile metal fizzogs. Oh, and they have no emotions. While this makes them useless contestants on reality TV (see REALITY TELEVISION) shows – when Fizz or Blowfly or whoever gets voted out and everyone starts weeping and all that, the robots just sit there, emotionlessly ticking – it is bloody good when it comes to heartlessly deciding that humans should no longer be running things, and that for our own good we should be mown down in our millions or made to lie on metal bunkbeds with electrodes feeding us reality TV shows.

So – getting to the point – surely they should have taken over by now? Lord knows they've had enough opportunities. But the problem is, robot-takeover-wise, that robots have proved themselves to be a massive disappointment. And it's not hard to see why.

Originally, robots were pretty exciting, if a little bit stupid-looking. Like Christmas trees, orphans and having steamy royal affairs with Scottish gamekeepers, robots first appeared in Victorian times. Although called boring stuff like 'mechanical men' and 'Mister Metalhurst', they were proper robots – that is, they were nine feet tall, made of iron and had faces. Soon they were given their proper name – 'robot' – after, of course, a Czech play, and then the future was theirs. Although most robot action took place – like the Korean War, hula hoops and having Martinis for breakfast – in the 1950s: robots were attacking people left, right and centre, and were set for a very exciting world takeover.

Sadly, all this turned out to be largely fictional. Real robots were a massive letdown. Instead of being nine feet tall, made of iron and having big eyes and grilles that shouted 'Danger, Will Robinson, danger!', they were designed to look as unthreatening, unexciting and

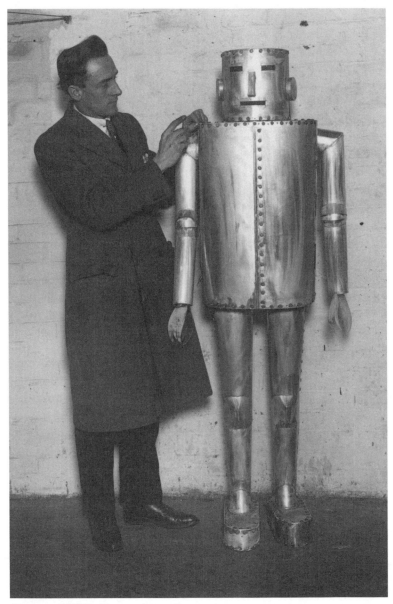

'Danger, Will Robinson, danger!'

un-fun as possible. Your average robot is just a big bendy arm that goes 'WHUHZEEEEE' and picks up some bolts – basically an anglepoise lamp on steroids. It's all rather depressing, really, and points to one of the real flaws of modern life.

Which is this: thanks to global warming and GM foods and experimenting on kittens and so forth, we have known for some time that science has been lying to us. What's depressing is that, as evidenced by this whole 'robots aren't going to be interesting' business, it now seems clear that science fiction has been lying to us as well.

ROBOTS 2
∿

A nother thing about robots, thinking about it, is that there are some that have legs and heads and make noises. But are they people? No, they're not. They're dogs. What is the point of making a robot dog? Doctor Who had a robot dog and it was tolerable because a) it didn't bark, b) it couldn't jump up and down or hump your leg because it didn't have any legs, and c) it could shoot people. In short, its three major attributes were sod-all to do with being a dog.

Admittedly, there are some robots that look like people, but the only ones that ever get in the papers are about four foot tall and for some reason are dressed up as those plastic spacemen you used to get in cereal packets. Which is no use to anyone. You want your humanstyle robot to look at least like some sort of tin butler, with a paintedon bow tie and shirt front. The only people who conceivably might want four-foot-tall plastic spacemen would be some giants who like surprise gifts in their enormous cereal. Which – given the limited likelihood of there being any such thing – hardly justifies spending millions of yen making robot spacemen.

THE RUSSIAN SPACE PROGRAMME
∿

C ome on – wasn't it a lot cooler than the American one? And yet it's been buried by history, neglected out of existence and airbrushed out of the records in a way that Stalin would have found impressive.

Meanwhile, every stateside gimp who could wear a space helmet without toppling off a gantry has been immortalized. Life isn't fair.

Here are a few reasons why the Russian space programme is the nuts:

1. **They put the first thing in space: Sputnik.** Admittedly it was essentially a bowling ball with some knitting needles in it, but while NASA was still trying to figure out how to do go-karts, Sputnik was flying above America, waving at cowboys and saying in Morse code, 'Hey, America! I can see down your top!'

2. **They put the first man in space: Yuri Gagarin.** America by now had figured out the go-kart but while they were painting MOON RASSER on the side, Gagarin flew round them again.

3. **Their astronauts were called 'cosmonauts'.** That just seems better somehow.

4. **Pencils.** Legend has it that NASA spent billions trying to invent a pen that wrote upside down in space. The cosmonauts took pencils.

5. **The Moon.** There are two urban myths concerning the Moon landings. One is that the Americans didn't go. Yawn. The other one is that the Russians DID go. And didn't tell anyone. Now that is stylish.

6. **Hungarians.** Only the Russians have put any Hungarians in space. And Germans and Czechs and Poles and probably a Frenchman. Americans have generally confined themselves to putting more Americans in space, which is greedy.

7. **Laika the space dog.** The first, and coolest, hero of space. Her name, brilliantly, means 'Barker'.

8. **Spacecraft.** American spacecraft are big and loud and shiny and frankly all vulgar and thrusting. Russian spacecraft look like they were made out of 1950s boiler parts and could blow up at any minute.

9. **And instead of being called weedy stuff:** like 'Apollo' and 'Gemini', like a gay sauna in South London, Soviet spacecraft were called tough-sounding spacey things like 'Soyuz'.

10. **Splashdowns.** American space capsules landed in the sea. Anyone can do that. Especially if there are helicopters and big aircraft-carriers to hold your hand. Soviet space capsules landed on land. Thud! Winner!

'Hey, America! I can see down your top!'

RUSSIA

~

And while we're at it, what the hell happened to Russia? They used to be evil but interesting, and also – and this is a good trick – boring and exciting at the same time. Evil and interesting because of, you know, the whole totalitarian regime thing, and the little badges and the cosmonauts (see THE RUSSIAN SPACE PROGRAMME). Boring and exciting because on the one hand the Soviet Union was grey and there was no food or decent telly, but on the other hand parades! Missiles! Banners! Spies! Not liking America! Threatening to start World War III. The Soviet Union was like a giant civil servant who took the train every day to the same office, did the crossword every morning and smelled a bit of sandwich spread, but every so often drank a bottle of whisky and told everyone in the world that he could kill them.

So we knew where we were with the Russians. They even had a great name. The USSR. That's like 'the USA' but with more and better letters. They had a better flag (see THE AMERICAN FLAG) and what they didn't know about marching past bulbous technicolor cathedrals wasn't worth knowing. Unfortunately, they spent so much time on the marching that they ran out of money and all the countries that they owned, like Poland and East Germany, said, 'Bugger this. We've seen *Miami Vice*. We have an incomprehensible and later-to-be-regretted desire to see Dire Straits in concert,' and tore down the Berlin Wall. Leaving the Russians to be just Russians.

This was all right for a bit, but then it went mental. And after it all settled down again, two sorts of Russians emerged. Gangsters – who are all very rich and live on ocean-liners and eat caviar and sometimes own sporting clubs around the world. And politicians – who don't own any sporting clubs but in every other respect are like gangsters. Hey! Satire.

HEALTH &
RECREATION

BINGE DRINKING

～

O r, as we call it in this country, 'being sociable'. Everything is relative, you know, and just because doctors and health ministers have no friends to go drinking with, they try and get their own back by claiming that the odd gallon is bad for us. Nonsense, the nation replies, my grandfather drank a lake of whisky every morning and he lived to be twelve.

But isn't there, as so often, an element of classism about binge-drinking coverage? Nobody ever complains when a lot of aristocrats or millionaires go out drinking; but some slightly tipsy girl falls through

'Slightly tipsy girl.'

the glass front of a chemist in Sunderland after 46 Moscow Mules and it's a Cause for Concern.

Interestingly, none of the opponents of binge-drinking has ever suggested an alternative. So how about it, Doctor Fun? Got any suggestions? Thought not. Two pints of Bacardi Breezer and a packet of wine then please, barman.

CREDIT CARDS
~

Didn't they used to be quite hard to get? Was there not once a time when, if you wanted a credit card, you had to fill out immense forms written out on vellum? Meanwhile teams of highly trained investigators turned your house upside down looking for evidence of unreliability and debt. And other teams of highly trained similar got your family and employers in a room and interrogated them until someone admitted that once you had borrowed 50p from them and forgotten to give it back.

Times have changed. These days 'getting into debt' is no longer a stigma. The very thing that gave our parents sleepless nights and moral dilemmas has, as a yardstick of behaviour, vanished into the ether. Debt is not only perfectly acceptable now, it's positively encouraged (is anything negatively encouraged?). And by whom is it encouraged? Banks, that's who. Credit-card issuers. You submit your accounts to them and do they say, 'Oh dear, you've been in debt, go away'? No. They say, 'Magic, you're always in debt. Have a massive credit limit and go and spend it all on cheap tat. Oh, and don't worry about the interest. You've got the rest of your life to pay it back. In fact, you'll have so much interest to pay back, you'll be dead before you can pay it all, so your kids will inherit it.'

Honestly, it's like they *want* us to get into debt.

PART WORKS
~

Part works are those magazines that want to be books that for some reason can only be sold in branches of WH Smith. Perhaps in the nineteenth century, WH Smith was out for a stroll with Prince Albert, possibly having a chat about the different merits of the *New Musical Express* and *Sounds*, when an assassin jumped out and fired at the Prince, and WH Smith leapt in front and took the bullet. Later Prince Albert promised Smith and his descendants that they would forever own the right to … But it seems unlikely.

What is for certain is that part works are very peculiar. They seem to be put together at random. One might be about World War I. One might be about knitting. Another might be about inland waterways. It makes no sense. Sometimes, to make things worse, there are combined part works. Knitting and weaving. Sailors and astronauts. Elephants and trains. It's as though some part-work king is sat at home, sticking pins into an encyclopaedia (see VIRTUAL ENCYCLOPAEDIAS) and shouting out random words to his assistant, Alaric.

Part works are always promoted in the same manner. They begin fantastically well, full of enthusiasm and excitement. There is a free gift – often of the highest quality and always designed to get the collector interested. A hand-detailed French Hussar of the Thirty Years. A pair of solid tungsten knitting needles. Hitler. The choices are well thought-out, and are mirrored by the contents of the maganiney thing itself. Lavish illustrations, beautifully rendered. Diagrams. Maps. Articles by the greatest experts in the land. And, best of all, issue two is free with issue one! For once the concept of Buy One, Get One Free (see 'BUY ONE, GET ONE FREE') works, because if you have got issue one of *Little British Soldiers*, then chances are that you actually want issue two.

The whole thing is, comparatively speaking, a panoply of majesty. Unfortunately, it all goes tits up when issue three comes out, two months late, with no free gifts and a slightly desperate ad on page six begging people to subscribe, with cash, right now. Then issue four comes out about a year later, with illustrations by a nine-year-old boy who's clearly scared of crayons, and that's it. Your favourite part work is never seen again, the only proof of its ever existing a small pile of back numbers in the garage and the realistic model of a French hussar taking pride of place in a starling's nest up the road.

SECOND-HAND BOOK SHOPS

❧

They're supposed to be cornucopias of delight – run by a little old man in gold-rimmed bifocals (see BIFOCALS) who sits at a wooden desk in fingerless gloves and exclaims, 'Ah! Pity to let this one go!' as you hand him a first edition of the Gutenberg Bible and a ten-shilling note. The shelves groan with affordable treasures from all eras of history, and there's even a chance that the extremely good-looking person over by the original James Bonds might nip back to yours for some booky sex. Of course, real second-hand book shops are not like this (but then, nothing is).

The first thing you notice when you go into one of these places is the smell. Old books stink. If they're not actually mouldy – and a mouldy, damp old book has the power to simultaneously depress the hell out of you and make your nose think that it has been transplanted to a deep, dark dungeon in medieval Russia – then they're almost certainly musty. Without wishing to be vulgar, old books smell like tree farts.

Once inside the shop, having put a hankie over your face to avoid both tree farts and dust, you can have a look at the books. There are three categories of second-hand book. There are the silly rubbish ones near the door. These are largely kept out for their covers, which are a bookseller's idea of funny, i.e. not funny. There's an old book of stories for girls whose title is vaguely and accidentally rude. There's a risqué 1950s paperback with a picture of a woman who is so busy smoking a fag that she hasn't noticed her breasts are making a run for it. And there's a book with a really long and boring title like *Potatoes and Hermeneutics: A Progress Report*.

The second category of book is the sort-of-normal book. Books you actually own. Books you've heard of. Books sold by book reviewers for gin money. These are no good, though; by some magic of economics they cost as much as a new edition of the same book and they are tattier. So you progress to the third category. Now this is more like it. A locked glass cabinet full of absolute classics. There's a first edition of the best book in the world. The other best book in the world sits next

'Old books smell like tree farts.'

to it, signed by the author. Behind that is a complete set of original eighteenth-century first editions of an author you've never read but who you know would look good in your library, if you had one.

You inch nearer, hoping to engage in a chat with the little old man in gold-rimmed bifocals. Sadly, he's not there because he retired in 1968. Instead, the shop is owned by a ginger ex-student who's still bitter about something that happened at college. He turns away from his fellow lit nerd and looks at you like you came to his birthday and used his cake as a lavatory. You ask to see a book in the cabinet. He laughs. The lit nerd laughs. The extremely good-looking person over by the original James Bonds laughs. You flee from the shop, never to return.

FREE CDs
~

Fortunately these are generally only given away with music magazines, which at least reduces the damage they can do. The people who compile free CDs to give away on the covers of magazines seem to believe that they are immune to one of life's golden rules: that anything free is rubbish. Large companies tend not to give away anything of value for the simple reason that if it was any good, they could get some money for it. However, the wide-eyed, innocent and presumably frequently mugged people behind the free CD thing do at least genuinely think that their buckshee product is good.

They begin by optimistically compiling a list of all the famous rock stars they'd like to appear on the album. Then, when all those people turn them down, they make a second list, this time of less famous rock stars they'd like on the album. After the people on this list turn them down, the process continues, until there is a new list of not-very-famous rock stars about whom the compilers wouldn't actually get upset if they saw their names on the CD case.

Now the process of getting songs from these people begins. The compilers would like, if not the act's last big hit, then something at least listenable. This is where the conflict really begins. The act's management are deeply reluctant to give away anything of value (see paragraph one) but they don't wish to totally offend the magazine giving away their product. So they cleverly find stuff that *sounds* like it might be.

Thus when the CD comes out it will feature one or more of the following:

1. A really good, very famous hit for the artist, but in a live version recorded in a pub with microphones apparently hooded by oven gloves.

2. A slightly less good and famous but actually quite cool lesser hit by the artist, but in a pointlessly remixed, or extended, or 'dub' version ('dub' in this case resembles not so much an incredibly cool Jamaican remix as just a regular song with the vocals taken off).

'The people who compile free CDs to give away on the covers of magazines seem to believe that they are immune to one of life's golden rules: that anything free is rubbish.'

3. A spectacularly pointless Beatles cover.

4. An exclusive track by the artist which has never before appeared on any other record. Because it's awful.

5. Some poetry, generally at the end of the CD, because otherwise you'd throw the CD out of your car window.

6. A bona fide classic song, not done live or remixed or buggered about with. Just also not done by the original artist, but by some indie act who thought it might be ironic to have a go at it.

7. As above, only done on the banjo, or with a string quartet, or any other unsuitable instrument.

8. A quite good song by someone you've never heard of.

9. A really bad song by someone you've never heard of.

10. A really awful song done by the son of someone who was huge in the 60s.

CULTURE
∽

When Margaret Thatcher said there was no such thing as society, she was wrong. There is society, fortunately, but what there isn't is culture. Which doesn't mean that we're all oiks nowadays and we don't like reading and pictures, just that the word 'culture' has become largely meaningless. It used to mean something quite big and grand, like the social, religious and artistic ties that bound us, but now it has a different meaning. Nowadays it means at best 'situation' – as in 'the culture of today' – and at worst 'thing'. But in the olden days, culture was a po-faced monolith that wouldn't let any books or music or art in if they were a bit common. Culture then was seriously daunting; listening to music meant having to sit through the whole of Wagner's *Ring Cycle* on a small wooden chair without any beer to drink. Reading meant volumes and volumes of Henry James without any pictures (say what you like about Charles Dickens – see CHARLES DICKENS – but at least his books had pictures).

Then it all changed. Some people noticed that several things in pop culture – The Beatles, commercial art, books that were fun – were as good as things in high culture, and so some pop-culture things were allowed into high culture, much like when a posh school lets in some of the brighter kids off the estate.

However, unlike the kids off the estate, pop culture refused to have its head flushed down the toilet or be called Oiky. Instead, it invaded high culture and took its place beside it. Which is all well and good, except now we have people saying things like, 'Westlife are equally as good as Beethoven,' and getting paid for it. Which can't be good.

INTERNET AUCTION SITES
∾

Invented by computers, probably, to provide work for other computers. eBay is, as everybody knows, a big online auction site where people put items up of any sort and other people bid for them. It may not be the world's only online site, but it seems to be the only one that anybody's ever heard of (don't write in).

eBay is, for the benefit of our lawyers, a wonderful place, and any remarks below are surely the merest speculation. That said, it seems to be extremely easy to lose your soul on eBay. Not literally, as some buffoon did try and auction his soul, and they wouldn't let him. Which is a shame, because it would have been top fun if the Devil had signed on and won the auction. Although that seems unlikely as, given the Devil's great age, he is unlikely to be terribly good with the internet.

No, the way of losing one's soul referred to is a less dramatic one. It's more the constant erosion of the psyche occasioned by what psychiatrists aren't but really should be calling the Crisis of Availability.

These days you can get anything online and, thanks to eBay, you can often get it really cheaply. Material items, that is. It's all very well trying to sell your soul online (there must be a web company who, unlike squeamish old eBay, would be very happy to flog the spirituous fabric of your being), but trying to buy a soul – now, brother, that's a different story.

We can buy anything we want on eBay (apart from weird stuff that's illegal and so forth – aren't lawyers great?) and so we do. Those Timpo knights in armour with the swivel heads and detachable swords? There's some. A complete set of Victorian hairbrushes in the original case? Sold to the ironic bald man at the back. And so on. The problem with this is that all the fun and the struggle (which, actually, is the fun) disappear when it's all so easy. There's none of the thrill of the chase, none of the satisfaction of finally tracking it down – you just win the auction and it's yours.

The only solution to this problem would be to either close down eBay and end its sheer lovely wonderfulness, or to have them occasionally just lie. You win that auction for the Action Man deep-sea diver in the original box and someone at the company sees that you've already got lots of Action Men (and you're 44), so they just write back and say, 'Sorry, we thought we had one, but it was a spaceman,' but they don't refund you, they just keep your money. And you keep your soul.

INTERNET AUCTION SITES 2
∼

The worst thing about the internet auction is that there is a horrible redundancy to it. A real auction, if memory serves, is a thrilling, loud, smelly event where people wave their arms and blow their noses and actually buy useful or interesting things, like cows, or houses. It's rooted in thousands of years of exciting history and is, essentially, both dramatic and practical.

The internet auction is neither of those things. It's largely a pointless exercise in filling up gaps in your past, twenty or thirty years too late. People go to auction sites, okay, sometimes to buy something useful, like a strimmer or a vast amount of wool, but mostly, generally and as a rule, to buy the things they never had as children. And these things, this being an affluent consumer society, are not love or comfort or water, but old toys.

There is something a bit wrong about a middle-aged man feverishly shopping for the seven *Star Trek* figurines he never got when he was a lad, or an Action Man deep-sea diver outfit even though his actual Action Man went to the jumble years ago. If, as was once said, cocaine is God's way of telling you that you have too much money, then buying a complete set of Power Rangers toys in the original blister packs is the universe's way of telling you that your life is simultaneously bloated and empty.

INTERNET SHOPPING
∼

It's got to be a bad thing. For a start it introduces us to options we don't want. Like substitution. Go online and buy some groceries from Killabusiness.com or someone similar. Do your shop. When the delivery comes, you will find that, unless you have ticked a little box, if they didn't have the thing you wanted – a pineapple, say – they have taken it upon themselves to make a substitution, one that they think is suitable. A can of rice pudding, say, or the *Tibetan Book of the Dead.* This is insane. When you're in a real supermarket, you don't suddenly think, Damn! No chicken pie with little peas in it! Oh well, these Lucozade-flavoured wine gums will do just as well. So when in a virtual supermarket (see 'VIRTUAL'), you don't want it either.

And the neither to that either is the vexing habit that many stores have of offering you more choices. They call them 'recommendations', because 'bloody stupid suggestions' is a bit too accurate. You buy six *Harry Potter* novels and they daringly venture that, if you liked them, you might possibly like the new one. What are, as they say, the chances of that being the case? Fairly high, probably. You purchase an album by rock band U2 and they suggest that you might like some other rock records by older men in leather trousers.

An entertaining, if expensive, way to while away your life and annoy some anonymous computer as it ticks away in some bunker in Silicon Valley is to do this: go online to a store where you have never bought anything before, and buy three completely different things. A disco album, say, a hairbrush, and a thingie for keeping your two-pound coins in. Then see if you get any 'recommendations'.

'If you liked "Best Disco Nights", and a hairbrush, and that two-pound coiny thing, you'll love ... er ... you'll love ... DOES NOT COMPUTE! DOES NOT COMPUTE! DAISY, DAISY, GIVE ME YOUR ANSWER DO!'

Might work.

INTERNET SHOPPING 2

∾

Then there's paying for it. These days we have became very distant from the golden age of rummaging for florins in a little leather purse and handing them over to the innkeeper or the ostler in a very reluctant manner. It's probably true that electronic credit transfer has made us careless with our money because we can't see it any more. Nevertheless, it still seems strange, given humanity's record for being suspicious and hostile to anything that a) involves money, and b) is new, that we seem quite happy to go online, buy a load of old rubbish that we don't really want and then – and then – give some complete stranger on a computer all our bank and credit-card details. Why? Because the computer says that this is a 'secure link'. This is, of course, the same computer that just asked us for all our bank and credit-card details – and we believe it when it says that our secret is safe with it.

This is madness. If an actual person did that, we'd be very worried and probably hit them. Yet when a computer does it – a computer probably wearing a big kipper tie, a trilby and with a jacket full of second-hand watches – we type in our payment details like we just don't care.

No wonder the machines haven't taken over (see ROBOTS). They don't have to. They're minted, the lot of them.

'BUY ONE, GET ONE FREE'
∽

This apparently generous offer is in reality a tool of the Devil designed to simultaneously tempt and annoy us. You're in the shop and have finally, after hours and hours of searching, found something that you actually want, or that fits you, or you haven't read, or isn't by Sting. You're about to buy the wretched thing so that finally you can go home, when you see it. The sticker. 'Buy One Get One Free'. Great. Now you have to begin the whole hellish process of shopping again, and chances are you'll just trundle around the gaff for an hour or two and then slowly start to lose the will to live, before putting back the one thing you have so far almost purchased, and leaving the shop feeling curiously suicidal. And then you get on the bus and suddenly remember exactly what it was you went into town to buy in the first place.

'THREE FOR TWO'
∽

This is similar to Buy One, Get One Free (see 'BUY ONE, GET ONE FREE') but somehow even worse. Because it channels you into an even more difficult trap – to save money (that otherwise you wouldn't even have thought about spending) you now find yourself looking around the shop for not one, not two, but three things you didn't really want in the first place. The fact that these three things you didn't really want in the first place only cost as much as two things you didn't really want in the first place is of little comfort as, once more, you trudge wearily home and fill your house with useless crudola.

'BUY ONE, GET ONE HALF PRICE'

∾

N°.

THE TOUR DE FRANCE

∾

Oh *mon Dieu*. Just what the world needs today. Thousands of Frenchmen on bicycles hurtling around Europe being annoying. And nowadays it's not just France, it's the Tour De Bloody

'Thousands of Frenchmen on bicycles hurtling around Europe being annoying.'

Everywhere. How would they like it if we went over there on our bikes and rode down their streets shouting, *'Allez sur le pavement!'*? Actually, they'd probably enjoy it, the contrary si-et-sis.

LIMOUSINES
∾

Stop it now. Just stop it. Nobody thinks that your limousine is full of rock stars or film idols. Because a) why would the Rolling Stones be stuck up a back street in Bury in their 'stretch', and b) Brad Pitt and George Clooney tend to go to the Oscars in vehicles that do not have cheap winking fairy lights glued onto the outside.

The only upside of the popularity of the stretch limo is that any foolhardy rock stars who do go cruising for show-off action in their over-priced El Dorado stretch limousines are inevitably ignored as everyone thinks they're a group of slappers from Rhyl.

HUMMERS
∾

The creepiest development in the history of motoring since the invention of the unlicensed minicab. Hummers, or humvees, were originally those big armoured-personnel carriers from the Gulf War which looked a bit like jeeps that thought they were ghetto-blasters. Designed specifically to carry people around so they could kill other people, hummers became incredibly glamorous to the kind of person whose intense consumption of steroids has caused his penis to disappear forever.

And soon they developed a slightly smaller hummer for 'civilian' use. Which is completely useless for normal life, takes up six blocks, is always driven by a git, and, in many ways, is just really unpleasant, like chrome-plating a Stuka and calling it a bouncy castle.

TOURIST BRITAIN
∾

Apparently Britain is now just one great big theme park. With no industry to speak of, we are best at making money out of just

'Britain is now just one great big theme park.'

being here and getting people to come and have a look. Actually, given that we are a cold, damp and hostile island where the food is vile and the entertainment positively Estonian, the tourist trade hasn't done a bad job at all.

But they're missing a trick. True, some people enjoy seeing the Trooping of the Colour and men in furry hats falling over. Agreed, we've got more ruined castles than anyone else. But there's more to this great nation than that! We've got no-go estates! Street crime! Armed youth! We should be in the adventure holiday market, not just the heritage market.

And why not combine the two? For just ten grand, you and the Queen have to keep control of Windsor Castle while it is besieged by the Sken Man Massive and other gangs off the Sun Hill estate. For even less, lead a party of Welsh Guards to a rave in Newcastle and see who survives! Go to the Tower of London and see if you can survive an episode of *EastEnders*! The possibilities are infinite, and cruel.

AMUSEMENT PARKS
~

O r whatever they're called. Another example of something we do badly, anyway. In America and probably some other, smaller, less loud nations, amusement parks are done well. You go in and you can almost hear the designers' voices, thinking about fun things and big things and ludicrous ideas. The best amusement parks are almost surreal in their excess, partly deranged in their cheerfulness and always exciting in their sheer imaginative drive.

In Britain, however, we still take as our standard the spinny-teacup roundabout. We occasionally splash out on a thing that goes up and down or round and round, but it's never a terribly thrilling one. And if we have a rollercoaster, it's not going to have a big sign on it saying THE BIGGEST ROLLERCOASTER IN THE WORLD! THRILLS GUARANTEED! In fact, it's probably not going to have a big sign on it at all, because nobody makes signs that say THE TENTH SMALL-EST ROLLERCOASTER IN WALES! SLIGHT ORANGE JUICE SPILLAGE GUARANTEED!

HELTER SKELTERS

∽

These days they mostly just turn up on the end of the pier, enabling parents with particularly squally children to hope that, instead of flying off the end of the slide onto a mat, the child will continue down the helter skelter into the sea, where it will fly into the mouth of a shark. Helter skelters are also one of the least aptly-named fairground attractions, because they do not so much hurtle you down and down like a metallic whirlpool, as let you slide slowly down in such a way that you might actually get stuck and have to wait for a fat bloke to ram you in the back to get you moving again.

DODGEM CARS

∽

The most significant thing about them are the signs telling you not to try and crash into other people. They're DODGEM cars, after all, not crashem cars or hitandrunem cars. But, of course, these signs are a blatant lie. The owners expect you to crash into other people. They want it. It's all part of the fun. Kids and teenagers love it.

The downside of this attitude is that when those same kids and teenagers start learning to drive, and the instructor says, 'Now, try not to hit anyone!', their subconscious mind goes, 'All right! It's rammin' time!'

THE GHOST TRAIN

∽

At first it's scary. Then you get older, and it's ridiculous. Finally, in later life, you go again, and the combination of cheap rubber monsters, eerily bad skeletons and that whole combination of mortality mocked and parody horror suddenly strikes you as an uncannily accurate portrait of the way fate and death mesh and interrelate. That's funfairs for you!

'At first it's scary. Then you get older, and it's ridiculous.'

THE COCONUT SHY
∽

The coconuts are glued on. You've got no chance. Try throwing the ball at the stall-keeper's head. As he reels round the place, moaning in Cockney, lean in and prise the coconut from the stall. It seems only fair.

ANYTHING CALLED 'WORLD' THAT
ISN'T AN ACTUAL WORLD
∽

So yes to Mars, no to 'AquaWorld'. Hurray for planet Earth, boo to 'World of Pirates'. We love Antares 7, we don't care for 'Trains' World'. Even Disney World is pretty horrible, and that's about as world-like as it gets. But your average British world is a shed with some damp models in it, and is closed on Sundays and Wednesdays. You don't see worlds like that on *Star Trek*.

MODERN LIFE

CONDITIONER

~

Makes no sense. Having invented a way of putting conditioner into shampoo – saving enormous amounts of effort, particularly for men, who would only want to take two bottles into the shower if they contained port – the hair-product people then decided to take it out again. Why not just go the whole hog and take all the ingredients out? Then we could all take into the shower some soap, some special eye-stinging chemicals and a basket of jojoba, and mix up our own shampoos on the spot.

AFTERSHAVE

~

Where did it go? When did they discover that men don't actually need to splash on some powerfully scented alcohol after a shave? Did some scientist, just seconds after putting on the Old Spice, think, Hang on – this stuff both hurts and smells, and seems to confer no medical benefits? Probably.

ANTIPERSPIRANT VERSUS DEODORANT

~

One of them stops you sweating, the other just covers it up. But which is right? They can't both be good. This isn't a case of horses for courses or different strokes for different folks. This is BO we're talking about here. We need someone from the big chemical firms to speak out and say, 'Okay, this is the deal. Antiperspirant seals up your pores and your skin dies,' or 'Deodorant just makes you smell of flowers AND sweat.' One or the other, please. We can take it.

BRITISH TEETH VERSUS AMERICAN TEETH

～

The orthodoxy of orthodontics. Americans are obsessed with our teeth. They use them as examples to scare their children with. 'If you don't wear a brace every day for the next fifteen years, floss, use interdental brushes and generally live your life as though you were actually WORKING FOR YOUR TEETH, you'll grow up to have British teeth.'

Because what could be worse than having not entirely symmetrical, not unnaturally white, characterless, denture-resembling great albino dominoes filling your mouth and making you look like someone jammed a white picket fence on top of your gums?

MOUSTACHES

～

Like baldness (see VOLUNTARILY BALD MEN), moustaches have been taken up by various male groupings – homosexuals, traffic wardens and people who keep meaning to join the Territorial Army. And, like baldness, moustaches are a slightly peculiar thing to want to have. You could understand if, say, Mr Ipkiss the scout master had grown a moustache the way some people grow a wart, and he hadn't got round to going into Boots and buying some moustache remover, but amazingly, he grew a moustache – and he did it deliberately.

BEARDS

～

Who decides where beards should begin and end? There really should be some sort of international standard. Some people have little jazz beards. Others cover their face in hair, leaving only a couple of gaps below the eyebrows for seeing out of. Some favour the chin beard. And some – the extremists of the beard world – go for the fringe-around-the-jaw look. This makes them feel really cool, until someone comes along and shouts, 'Oi! Mister Upside-Down Face! Nark it!' or something equally colloquial.

'Oi! Mister Upside-Down Face! Nark it!'

'Who decides where beards should begin and end?
There really should be some sort of
international standard.'

WIGS
∾

L ook around you! Everyone's bald! It's okay! (See VOLUNTARILY
BALD MEN.)

SIZE ZERO
∾

W hile naturally one deplores the sight of idle human heifers
thumping around the shopping centres of the world, creating a
massive canvas shortage as they demand more and more acreage of

jeans to be run up for their super globular bums, the opposite case is, inevitably, just as sickening.

Models, as you may have noticed, are not good role, er, models. Leaving aside the whole issue of whether or not they're actually human in the conventional sense of the word – for most of them seem to have bypassed the whole sentient consciousness and having-a-brain business, which will make them valuable weapons should we ever go to war with Mars – there's their lifestyle. They smoke. They drink. They take drugs. They eschew normal language and talk like Cockneys who have recently received a savage beating. They wear the kind of make-up that previously had only been seen on the sides of ships during World War II. And they don't have any dinner, ever (see PEOPLE WHO SAY, 'I JUST EAT WHAT I WANT ALL THE TIME AND I NEVER PUT ON ANY WEIGHT, I DON'T KNOW WHY').

And so it seems only sensible that young girls should take their cue from these razor-cheeked monsters. Never mind that these children are still growing, mentally and physically. Never mind that the examples offered by the modelling profession are both freakish and wrong. Models don't care. The only reason they might not want some young girl to mimic them and lose weight to a bodily damaging degree is because the one thing they really fear is some younger model coming along and displacing them from the pratwalk.

THE GYM
∿

There was a period in human history, incredibly, when we didn't need gyms. True, we had them, but they were first used by slightly dodgy ancient Greeks who, if the vases are to be believed, liked to run around in the nud with helmets on. Then time passed and gyms were used solely by PE teachers for the purpose of humiliating young boys and girls.

But since the 1980s, the gym has risen to a new and slightly peculiar prominence. For a start, women got involved. Thanks largely to the invention of leggings, leotards and headbands, going to the gym began to seem less like something the Kray Twins would do on their lunch-break and more like something that girls might want to do.

At the same, men became more body-conscious, or 'gay', to use the technical term. Both proper homosexuals and men who just fancied themselves naked started to use gyms. Things like jogging and aerobics were invented to make fitness even more exciting. Televisions were installed, which showed MTV videos where people in leggings and leotards sang songs about being fit.

Surely this is all a good thing? Well, yes and no. For a start, consider if you will the concept of fitness. As with most animals, it used to be a by-product of daily activity – running from predators, surviving on a diet of basic nutrition, stealing eggs from nests, and so forth. But these days we tend not to do any of those things in our daily lives (unless we see a particularly tasty egg). We sit at desks, we sit in cars and planes, we sit in bars and restaurants, and we do, in short, bugger all apart from sitting. So – instead of having a special place where we go to get fit we should just accept our physical fate, get really fat and have robots trundle us around everywhere in wheelbarrows (see ROBOTS). It is our clear destiny.

CHANGING ROOMS
∿

If you do go to the gym, against all the laws of nature, there are certain things that you really will not enjoy. One is the changing room. No matter how much money your trendy health club has spent on tiling and video monitors and really nice soap, the changing room is essentially no different from the ones you used at school. It's wet, damp, and full of towels and really oddly-shaped people. Admittedly, these days total strangers are less likely to flick you with wet towels or make comments about your anatomy. But it's still pretty weird in there. Largely because you are still forced to look at people in the nude. Which, despite what art and porn may tell us, is rarely pleasant.

Especially if these people enjoy shaving in places you never thought people shaved.

GRUNTING
~

The real worst thing about gyms. Some people – let's call them prats – feel that, when working out, they have to make a lot of noise and do a lot of rhythmic grunting. This incessant commentary of guttural body noises can sometimes be very disturbing, as it sounds exactly like you have been trapped in a forest full of obscene phone callers.

CLASSES
~

You were tempted by joining a class – aerobics, pilates, jazzercise – because one day as you struggled downstairs to use some machine or other and wondered how bored you could be in one hour, you saw them. A vision through the glass. Lithe young men and women, making practised, rhythmic moves in front of mirrors, with a friendly, assured and attractive teacher. Even the music was quite pleasant. So you joined.

Halfway through the first session, something snapped in your kidneys and you had to sit down. You've never been back.

MEMBERSHIP
~

As we all know, the greatest financial trick of all time. Everyone joins the gym on New Year's Day, determined to shed that Christmas flab and make a new person of themselves. And then something snaps in your kidneys, or you just forget to go, or you can't find your towel, and you never go back. But you've paid for a year's membership.

The only solution to this is to actually go to the gym and get fit, or to use it as a sort of gentlemen's club, and sit on the benches with a copy of *The Times* and a large brandy. It might work.

OPTICIANS
∽

They used to be fun. You had the big card, the funny clacky lens thing, the light in the eye, and that slightly spooky part where you could hear the air whistling into the optician's nostrils. You had free eye tests. You could get John Lennon glasses for about ten pence. But now all that has changed.

For a start, they charge for everything, from test to specs. And there aren't even any old copies of *Punch* to pass the time. The eye tests are ultra modern and confusing and you keep thinking you might actually fail your test and not be allowed to see any more. They puff air in your eyes and claim it didn't hurt. And then you go upstairs and everything costs a million quid and all the glasses look like something out of *Speccy Designer Murderer Weekly*.

The whole thing is horrible. Opticians have become, effectively, dentists of the eyes.

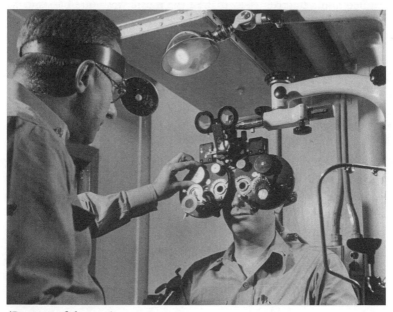

'Dentists of the eyes.'

BIFOCALS
∾

Specifically designed to make people feel old. Bifocals – or to give them their new, postmodern name, varifocals – are, as you probably know, sort of double-decker spectacles with one lens up top for looking at normal stuff like women and clouds, and one lens below for reading. The problem is that the human eye isn't used to this sort of ocular apartheid, and keeps making you fall downstairs onto the human arse.

Worse, bifocals still seem to be created by librarians and antique dealers, with lots of gold, frames designed for twinkling over the top of, and arms just begging to have a loop of colourful thread attached to them.

CONTACT LENSES
∾

Their sole purpose is to make people look mental. A long-term spectacle-wearer who switches to lenses will find that their eyes look simultaneously wider and more squitty. Worse, the eyes will dry up and, when they're not doing that, the lens will scuttle over the surface of the eye like a round, invisible crab. And then it takes three hours to take them out, clean them, and put them in again. No wonder people like laser eye surgery (see LASER EYE SURGERY).

LASER EYE SURGERY
∾

One of the many things that the Russians invented, like wooden teeth and space travel (see THE RUSSIAN SPACE PROGRAMME). Laser eye surgery works in the exact opposite way to going to the opticians. Opticians simply add extra layers of lenses to your eyes to improve your sight. Laser surgeons simply peel layers off your eyes to expose stronger eye magic below, or something. Quite frankly, nobody knows how laser eye surgery works, because everyone who's ever had it explained to them has run screaming from the room before the mad scientist explaining it to them has finished.

REFUSE
◝

Aptly named, if it's just written down. But not aptly named if you say it, because 'refuse' as in 'say no to' and 'refuse' as in 'rubbish' are pronounced differently. Still, this is a book, so it works, sort of. Anyway. Refuse has become one of the great issues of late, because councils have finally found a way of dealing with the whole problem of waste collection: namely, not doing it at all. It's ingenious, really. By reducing the amount of rubbish collections from 'frequent' to 'hardly ever', our magnificent elected representatives (we voted for 'em! And if you didn't vote, you should have voted for someone else – anyone else) have found an ecologically sound solution to an age-old conundrum. Now the person responsible for dealing with the rubbish is the person who created it! It's genius! Now we have to decide ourselves – shall we learn how to recycle our waste and thereby save the planet, or shall we just let it pile up, rotting and vile, and just hope that someone else sorts it out for us.

Actually, thinking about it, it seems unlikely that Ladbrokes will be taking bets on this one.

POST OFFICE COLLECTIONS
◝

Like the bins (see REFUSE), the mail has also been curtailed to an absurd amount. However, it's even more vexing in the case of the post because, unlike the mail, the bins were never collected three times a day in the past. Because amazingly, or boringly, depending on who you're talking to, decades ago you could write a letter to a lady in the morning, asking if she'd like to come round and admire your penny-farthing, and by four o'clock that afternoon the postman would be delivering you a letter from her dad, threatening you with a horse-whipping. Nowadays you're lucky if your letter even gets past the nailed-up slot in the letterbox, let alone actually delivered to someone's house.

This must be hard for the poor postmen. With the old delivery system they were as fit as a fiddle, running from house to house trying to keep up with the constant stream of letters. The way things are now, they must just sit there, bored out of their minds. What they need is inspired leadership from the top! But they're not going to get any. It seems astonishing that, of all the agencies in this modern world radically changed by communication, the one least equipped or willing to change is the one in charge of written communication. You'd think the Post Office would rise to the challenge – competing with emails, delivering letters by the second, introducing a new and even more efficient parcel post – but no. They've just continued to be as useless and uninspired as they've always been. We should just be grateful that the Royal Mail aren't in charge of emails: *'Dear Sir, we're sorry but you weren't in when we tried to deliver an email this morning. So we have dropped it in next door's bin.'*

THE END OF SHOPS
❧

Soon everything will be online. So they tell us, although nobody seems quite clear as to exactly how they're going to fire chickens and beer and naked women out of our computers into the living room. This is supposed to be a good thing, because everything is always supposed to be a good thing, but like all supposed good things, it's probably not.

Admittedly, it's hard to feel sorry for shopkeepers. These are people who have two mottos – NO MORE THAN TWO THIEVING KIDS IN THE SHOP AT ONE TIME and GIVE ME MORE MONEY – but even shopkeepers have to earn a living. And the great thing shopkeepers have that internets don't is shops. Actual, real shops, with stuff in that you can go and look it, and lift up, and squeeze, and read, and so on. When you buy something in a shop, you are buying the actual object that you wanted. When you shop online, you are buying a real-life version of a jpeg and the real-life apple or CD might be markedly inferior to its online pictorial equivalent.

There's also the issue of the big old world out there and physical space. With inner-city decline, and so on, we've already seen lots of thriving city centres turn into shuttered-up slums. If internet shopping really kicks in, and some men with glasses say that's what's going to happen, then this closure of stores will spread. And in the twenty-first century, that closure doesn't just mean Mister CD or Alan the Grocer. It means the mega-malls. Those converted quarries outside town full of stores and boutiques and fast fooderies will become ghost settlements, three-storey elevator-connected graveyards. Even the massive Tesco and Sainsbury's super-stores and their brutal ilk will empty, as people shop from home, and soon all your Nectar card will get you is bitten by a pack of wild dogs as they snuffle round the deserted fish and meat section.

Let's hope so, anyway.

'ACADEMIES'
∼

Or an example of how control freaks really do need control. Not content with establishing chairs of business, not content with ensuring that universities these days are essentially factories for turn-ing out business executives, some senior corporate types have set up their own academies. You know, just in case the MassiveCorp-sponsored course on Business Management and No Arts Content At All might accidentally be infiltrated by community playwrights. Vanity and insecurity are not the best foundations for a place of education. Unless, of course, it's a stage school (see ACADEMIES FOR THE PERFORMING ARTS).

THE FAR LEFT
∼

We miss them. Not as the irritant they so often could be, all long words and being angry, and splitting into splinter groups every five seconds, and being a place where trendy actors (see ACTORS) could put on uniforms and play at revolution. But as a lot of people who, by and large, did at least mean what they said, and did think that a revolution would be a good thing, and that things could be better if we all had an equal slice of the cake, and that sort of thing. But now they're gone, because they were too closely associated with nasty regimes and shouting and guns, and because they were a bit short on laughs. Still, with the world the way it is, a mess of dubious former communist countries (see RUSSIA), pants-off naked aggressive capitalism disguised as consensus, oh, and the return of the far right (see THE FAR RIGHT), we sort of need them. If only there was a kind of left-wing Drake's Drum we could beat, that they might return to us, waking from their tombs in Avalon, banners flying and donkey jackets tightly buttoned up, coming to, if not save us, then give us a thorough leafleting.

THE FAR RIGHT
❧

An old and reliable visitor to these shores. Despite the fact that all far-right parties are not in the least ideological, or morally sound, or even possessed of the tiniest amount of usefulness, sense or anything that wouldn't make a sane adult vomit at the mere thought of them, they're still with us. Despite the fact that only the most moronic government would allow conditions to exist where their particular vileness can flourish, they're back. And despite the fact that scientists have now proved that everyone who has ever led a far-right party is in fact directly descended from something a monkey did down the side of a tree when it was frightened, we still let them into our schools and homes. We should send them all back, it's the only language they understand.

COMPREHENSIVE SCHOOLS
❧

Once a badge of courage for millions, who could say 'I went to a comprehensive' and imply in those few short words that they had spent their lives living among the hardest of hard cases, struggled to learn to read and write in classrooms pockmarked from constant Uzi fire, and only through the most extraordinary application and talent escaped to somehow become one of the directors of a company owned by their dad.

Comprehensives get a hard time these days, possibly because teaching lots and lots of kids in huge classrooms on a low budget isn't the most efficient way to get them through exams. On the other hand, it does at least – to use a popular phrase – 'prepare them for real life', in that real life is not only crowded out with people who don't like you or care if you live or die, but if you hang out with enough people who are as bored as you are, you might learn how to make your own fun.

GRAMMAR SCHOOLS
◡

They feel like they are the oldest forms of school in the world. Certainly they're more authentic-sounding than public schools (see PUBLIC SCHOOLS), which increasingly look more like a cross between Hogwarts and a holding cell for space aliens. Grammar schools are very odd places; predicated on the eleven-plus system, they purport to be designed to educate bright kids, children who didn't deserve to go to the metalworky factory prep that is secondary school.

And the new grammar-school boy or girl would turn up, cap on head and satchel reeking of leather, confident that this brave new world (see *BRAVE NEW WORLD*) of education would propel them into some thrilling position of power and importance. Because, at twelve years old, they didn't know that all the positions of power and importance had been reserved for some different children, and in the end, a grammar school was a place that taught you how to be a better accountant.

PUBLIC SCHOOLS
◡

What can be said about public schools that hasn't been said a thousand times before? Nothing, so let's say it all again. Their 'traditions' are mostly lies and rubbish, invented a few decades ago to give them spurious weight and importance, and also to shore up the dubious idea that, just because something is old, it is also good. Their uniforms are the same, faked-up dress-up nonsense with straw hats and comedy collars. The Latin hymns? The weird rules about not walking down Coghills when it's Mother's Day? The same. Public schools, weirdly, act as theme parks for themselves, reiterating made-up histories and legends for fun and profit.

Their excellence is based on enormous financial injections; their superiority entirely related to feudalism, which is always a good way to

'Their uniforms are … nonsense.'

run a modern nation. Their food is disgusting. Their sexuality is at best enforcedly gay and at worst paedophilic. And their pop groups are always crap.

On the other hand, the *Jennings* books are absolutely brilliant.

'EXPRESS' AND 'LOCAL' SUPERMARKETS
∾

Not content with wrecking the economies of thousands of towns and villages around the country with their enormous ranchy-roofed superstores – which also destroy the environment by making everyone drive hundreds of miles into the countryside just to buy some loo roll – the big supermarket chains (are there any small supermarket chains?) have now decided, like the awful oppressors that they are, to take over everywhere. Even places where there's no room for a supermarket.

This is where the little supermarkets come in. Not your traditional Spar and Fine Fare, which were quite cute and dinky when one thinks about it, with their garish aisles full of frozen peas and their proper 60s muzak. (Not that trendy triphop muzak we get nowadays, this was the full-on, undilutable real stuff. Anyway.) No, we're talking 'Metros' and 'Express'es and 'Locals', horrible little miniaturized versions of your actual Big Bugger real supermarket. Except that, as if to mimic the corner store that it has now replaced (see BUTCHERS REPLACED BY BUTTON SHOPS), it doesn't have a very wide range of goods.

BUTCHERS REPLACED BY BUTTON SHOPS
∾

And so on. Useful shops replaced by completely blooming useless shops. A grocer that's now a kite shop. An ironmonger's that's now the premises for a wargaming supply store. And so on. A quick stroll through any town nowadays suggests that, not only do we have too many silly shops, but that surely Armageddon is well overdue.

EUROPE
∾

What happened? Europe used to be this place that either we went on holiday to or they invaded us. Now they've suddenly got really full of themselves and are telling us what to do all the time. It's ridiculous. These are the people whose very languages are so duff that they have to speak English to each other just to buy shoes. (Although, to be fair, it's not real English, it's American English. You know, the export version.) These are the people who famously communicate either by jabbering or war. They have a weird religion, which is like the Church of England only with more frocks and perfume. And, strangest of all, they hate us. Granted, everyone hates us, but that's not the point. These people used to be scared of us.

Thanks to some treaties and stuff, though, Europeans are no longer scared of us. In fact, legally, they can tell us what to do. This can't be right. Just because we agreed to be subject to a largely rational system of laws and ideas that are much more far-reaching and libertarian than our own doesn't mean that everyone in Europe isn't a parade-crazy dictator-lover.

EU RULINGS
∾

Yes, they are frequently mental. Then again, has anyone actually SEEN one of these things in practice? Because while certain papers (see TABLOIDS and POSH TABLOIDS) are constantly running stories about how a man in Kenilworth was ordered to be crucified because he said the word 'England' or how some shillings were hanged for treason in Strasbourg, and so forth, daily life hasn't been much affected. The most high-profile case was the one where the EU said it was actually perfectly fine to sell things by the pound.

While it's certainly wrong to impose excessively silly rulings on the lovely people of Britain, one has to reflect on this: if the whingeing anachronists who want St George's Day and guineas and all that back had their way, we'd still be spending groats and measuring in rods and furlongs. So shut it.

SUPERSTAR ADOPTIONS
∾

A very noble thing. The superstar adopts a child from a poor country for the noblest of reasons, and it's a coincidence that they've got a flop movie coming out that week, or that there are lots of press around when the adoption takes place. And doubtless the child will be well cared for, and its parents will always be around, and will no way leave the kid in the limo by mistake when they're off for a mad one in a nightclub.

SUPERSTAR ADOPTIONS 2

∽

The vexing thing about them, as is sometimes pointed out by the representatives of charities and the developing country (see DEVELOPING COUNTRIES), is that superstars always assume that the life they can give the child is innately superior to the life it would have had with its own family, in its own surroundings, in its own country. Perhaps they are right. Then again, given that most rich famous people are barmy, and their kids are even worse, it might make more sense to introduce a reverse adoption process, where the children of famous people are brought up by peasant farmers in Malawi. Makes a lot more sense.

PETITIONS

∽

Another modern irritant. While it's a good thing, probably, that some road doesn't get built or someone is freed from jail, and so on, the least effective method for achieving any of this must surely be the petition. Doubtless in simpler times, when the Prime Minister got a huge great piece of paper with ye signatures of ye masses appended to it, he used to brick it and think, Crap! They're all against me. I'd better release this road or abolish this tree or whatever it is they want.

But these days politicians are a lot more sophisticated. They get the email addresses of all the people who signed the petition and have them shot. Probably. Except for the ones who signed themselves 'Mickey Mouse' or 'Donald Duck'. These they simply report to the Disney Corporation, who sue them for millions of dollars.

Not really! Politicians are always listening out for the voice of the public, because they love us. Keep signing petitions, everyone, because we can all feel good that we signed something and that way we don't have to actually do anything hard, like leave the house.

LETTERS TO NEWSPAPERS
❧

They're all annoying. There are six basic types of letters to newspapers:

1. **The really angry letter.** 'If James Bumchoff really thinks that immigrants are good for the country, he should come to our village, where a foreigner once sold me some bread that was a bit stale!' These really are still written by colonels and armed lesbians.

2. **The whimsical letter.** These generally end in a stupid question, like, 'Last week my postman failed to deliver any mail to my door whatsoever. Is this a record?', or 'During the war I was made to eat nails and never once complained. Could any modern child say the same thing?' The answer to all these questions should always be, 'Who gives a broken toss?'

3. **The tiresome real-life anecdote.** 'In 1968, my wife and I holidayed on what is now the island of Nince in the Bay of Crabs. We found we had no lightbulbs ...' and so on for about a week until the conclusion, which is always a sort of 'um-HUM' finger-pointing bit of nonsense like, 'I very much doubt that today's doctors would agree with this.'

4. **The baffling non-sequitur.** 'Your editorial "Socks are Good" claimed that socks are warm in winter. How then does he explain the colour of tomatoes?'

5. **The PR self-defence (see PR PEOPLE).** 'Last week an article about Happy Cheeses claimed that Happy Cheeses were toxic and made people explode. In fact this is a lie, and even if it did happen that one time, that wasn't the cheese's fault, and even if it was, it was an accident, and anyway, look up there, a big spider!'

6. **The petitioning letter.** Like a petition (see PETITION) but with fewer names and a bit more famous. These are always signed by the same twenty-seven people, three of whom are theatrical (i.e. not real) knights (see KNIGHTS).

'MARKETING'

෴

If someone says to you, and God forbid they ever will, 'Hi! I'm in marketing,' run like hell. Because there is no such job as marketing. Unless you actually own some markets, marketing is a meaningless term. The people who 'work' in marketing turn up every day with a big coffee in their fat hands, hang their jackets on the back of their chairs, and start phoning people. The people they are phoning also 'work' in marketing. And so it goes on, a redundant waltz of horror.

Ask someone in marketing to tell you exactly and precisely what it is they do for a living and they will burst into flames. Guaranteed.

LOGOS

෴

The modern equivalent of flags, logos are quite the thing nowadays. Everyone from trainer manufacturers to some teenage wannabe rock star on MySpace has got one. And the weird thing is, the less expensive and famous a logo is, generally the better it is. A mad rapper in his bedroom? He's got a little record with his initials on it. The designer of the 2012 Olympics logo? They've got 45 squidillion pounds and obviously the sight of so much money made them so terrified that they panicked and made a logo that's better suited to a campaign for the promotion of vomit.

LEYLANDII

෴

'Hedges from Hell'. That was the slogan. Because if you really want to replicate the experience of burning in the eternal flames of damnation, surely the best way is to plant some conifers and not trim the tops. You do wonder what these people would do if they actually went to the real Hell. 'Hell from Hell' doesn't quite have the same ring to it.

Anyway. The golden age of the 500-foot-tall tree may sadly be over, as legislators – weak-kneed and slow when it comes to ending poverty, war and famine – have stepped in to end one of the minor storms in a lovely Wilton teacup of recent years. Bloody great big trees. Of course, they only become bloody great big trees if their owner doesn't shin up a ladder and trim the tops off every now and then. But, as he or she has planted the buggers in the first place because they grow very tall, very fast, and give them some privacy, that's unlikely to happen. Hence the trouble.

Said trouble is of course typical. Because this is a nation of people obsessed with 'privacy'. And, by the way, the same people who are quite happy to have other folk fingerprinted and ID-carded and filmed by CCTV are, of course, the first ones to go mental when someone can see into their back garden. They are, in short, the very people who gave the world the concept of an Englishman's home being his castle in the first place.

It's something of a paradox. No to the Euro, a universal currency which enables us a) to work out how much things cost around the continent, and b) to make Americans feel small. But also no to big, privacy-making trees whose only crime is to reduce the amount of sun in the English garden. Of which, of course, there is normally loads. These same people, by the way, wouldn't generally object to a vast amount of shade over their gardens if it was created by a 40-foot flagpole with an enormous flag of St George on top.

And what's wrong with blokey next door – who, you always get the impression from the enraged articles in the paper, has only recently traded his horse and caravan for bricks and mortar and is a stranger to both hot water and the written word – wanting a bit of privacy? You don't want to see him stripped to the waist, mowing the lawn and drinking cider from the barrel at the same time. And he doesn't want to see you either.

BENDY BUSES

∾

Once upon a time, there was the Routemaster bus. It was brilliant. People who didn't live in London would travel in by dogcart and Hoppa to see this wondrous charabanc as it cruised the busy streets like a mighty red yacht. Passengers hopped on and off like happy sparrows, and the conductor waved them goodbye, having first collected their fares and told them they could put their parcels in the weird boxy space thing under the stair.

But one day London elected a mayor whose sole mission was to rid London of pigeons and Routemaster buses. In the first instance, he was unsuccessful, as London is also the place where mad old biddies go, armed with bread and black dresses, to keep the pigeons fed. Sadly, no such luck befell the Routemaster, as its only vocal fans were quiet middle-aged men who liked to write down serial numbers and secretly preferred slippers to sex.

So the Routemaster went, and it was replaced, not by a big old chunky double-decker, but with the Articulated Bus. In this case, the Articulated Bus is called a Mercedes Benz Citaro, but the city as one revealed a talent for spotting the obvious and nicknamed the Citaros 'bendy buses'. Which, in the circumstances, was quite kindly, as a better name might be 'bendy bus that has been known to burst into flames and is great for fighting and fare-dodging'.

The Citaro is possibly one of the most questionable ideas in the history of transport. So far there have been two strong arguments for its retention. Firstly, it is new. The logic of this argument is that new things are good because they are fresh and exciting. And the wheels fall off old things. It doesn't take into account the fact that, very soon, the Citaro will be old (or, if it bursts into flames, a shell). The second argument is that there is better access for disabled people and the elderly. This is true, but doesn't explain why someone can't just incorporate good access onto a real bus.

They can't, however, do anything about the streets. Bendy buses are too big for cities. In Leeds, one of them whacked a cake shop with its bus arse. In London, routes had to be changed to suit the buses, which is useful. Then there's the fare-dodging element. Now even morbidly obese people wearing luminous hats can fare-dodge because the driver is at one end and the door is at the other. (This was also the case with the Routemaster, but they had conductors. Presumably employing people to do useful jobs is less sensible than sacking them to not save money in the long run.)

But fare-dodging is less of an issue (it's also fun if you can get away with it, and it might cause London Transport, or Immodium, or whatever they're called this week, to go bust). The worst thing is that, without a conductor, and with a big old space to run round in, there's the whole violence issue. At best, bendy buses are slow, ponderous, wall-breakers. At worst, it could be argued that they're a fire trap with a driver at one end and a knife fight at the other.

IMMIGRATION
❧

Apparently a very bad thing. They come over here, taking our jobs, and so forth. How do they manage that? They have, it seems, British passports. Which they became somehow entitled to by being born in countries that used to be British. Said countries became British by lots of soldiers and merchants going out there in the old days, taking people's jobs, killing them, and so forth. It's a sort of very slow Newtonian thing.

Oh, and nothing beats Americans called Katzenberg, Reilly, Smith, Fratelli, MacDonald or Vishnovski complaining about 'foreigners' coming over the border into their country. Let's see some Cherokees get put in charge of immigration. That would be fun. Send the *Mayflower* back!

LIVING IN THE REAL WORLD
❧

Possibly the most irritating dimwad expression ever. 'Time to live in the real world, buddy,' as they say at important business events. 'He's just not living in the real world,' people say about someone whose ideas are perhaps a little unusual, or nuts. While this is a useful yard-stick for anyone who has the power to travel between the real world and some parallel, fictional worlds, it's more of a hindrance in every other circumstance. Because, despite what the bozos using this cliché may think they mean, what they actually mean by 'the real world' is 'inside my dull brain'. Which is neither a world nor particularly real.

ID CARDS
∾

One of the things that separates us from people whose lives are like old spy films – i.e. the rest of the world – ID cards are surely no fun. Wherever you go, whatever you do, you have to carry what looks like proof of membership of a Jupiter slave gang with you. This feels a bit demeaning, and besides you might lose it and have to pay a fine.

ID cards are rubbish because they tamper with our illusion of freedom. It doesn't matter that we're fingerprinted, irised up (see IRISES), driving licensed and cross-referenced on every computer and CCTV camera between the two poles, it's a ball and chain too much to give us ID cards as well. They might just as well give us barcodes on our wrists. 'Dawn! Can I get a price check on a Kevin Thompson?'

IRISES
∾

And that finger thing at the airport. The fact that we cannot visit our trusted friends in America, on whose side we have gone to war quite a lot lately, without having a thorough security check, is more than a bit annoying.

'Hello, I'm on your side, apparently.'

'Take your trousers off, Limey, and sit with those terrorists.'

'What, the Perkins family from Leicester?'

And so on.

AIRPORT SECURITY
∾

The war against terror, we're told, is a matter of out-thinking the bad guys. Thinking the unthinkable. Being One Step Ahead at all times. It's a good theory. In practice, if airport security is a good example, it consists entirely of banning things after they've been thought of. Anyone who really wanted to cause chaos at an airport should ring up and claim that they have invented an exploding passport. Or poisoned a fat bloke from Essex with a Big Mac. Or checked in a luggage item filled with piranhas. Or anything that you commonly find at an

'Anyone who really wanted to cause chaos at an airport should ring up and claim that they have invented an exploding passport.'

airport which somehow no 'Thinking the Unthinkable' security person has yet got around to thinking of before someone else.

Then again, going through a metal detector with no shoes, belt, water or nail scissors does at least add some substance to the eternal feeling you have upon going on holiday that you've forgotten something.

SMIRTING

One of those many slang phrases that nobody actually uses (see SLANG TERMS IN THE DICTIONARY), 'smirting' is a particular idiot child in the simpleton world of made-up colloquialisms. It is a combination of the words 'smoking' and 'flirting', and is meant to describe this apparent thing where people who go outside in the street to have a fag see someone else having a fag and start – you guessed it – flirting with them.

'Hello, I see that you are smoking. My, how desirable you are.'

'Yes, I too find your Bensony complexion alluring. Let's get married.'

It's possible but not very likely. Most people smoking outdoors are too cold and nauseous to be overcome with desire. Beside, surely 'floking' is a much better word for it.

SLANG TERMS IN THE DICTIONARY
∾

In their headlong rush (is there any other kind of rush? A footlong rush sounds like something an otter would order in a sandwich bar) to look modern and contemporary, the old boffins who compile dictionaries are always cramming in as many modern slang phrases as possible.

This is a pity. For a start, it's against the original spirit of the great dictionaries. Reacting against the prototype of Doctor Johnson, whose dictionary was essentially a lot of headings with smart-arse remarks underneath them (not that there's anything wrong with that), a lot of men in little round tasselled hats sat down and decided to make the writing of a dictionary the most plodding, dull and precise process imaginable. They would write new and old words down on bits of filing cards, find references from books, cross reference them with the cards, and build up a case, as it were, for the word's existence and provenance. For a word to get into the dictionary was harder than getting a ladybird into the SAS.

But in the twenty-first century, dictionaries pretty much have their knickers around their ankles, figuratively speaking. Dictionary compilers are so desperate to look cool, so keen to get mentioned in the Sunday papers, that they'll put words in their new edition that nobody actually uses but were probably made up by some newspaper columnist or drugged-up tramp. And these words and phrases build up like vocab barnacles, never to be scraped off. Phrases like 'smirting', for example (see SMIRTING). Short-lived TV catchphrases. Really important etymological stuff like that.

TOWNS
∾

Not what they were, which is lovely big things with walls around them and markets and later on some industry, making cars or tea-towels. These days towns are there to do what? Put shops in the middle of and surround with people who don't want to live in the towns because they're a bit unpleasant. And so all the shops in the town die and the people move even further out and then the town gets worse, until in the end it reverts to a primitive state and goes to war with Exeter.

TOWNS 2
∾

Oh, a common criticism of towns is that nowadays they're all identical, apparently. Because they have the same shops, you see. Well, boo hoo. For a start, this has been going on for donkeys, as anyone who's ever seen a recreation of some Roman city or main street in Babylon will know. And ever been stuck in some tedious, 'properly preserved' cathedral town? Wow. They're all the same as well, you know. Cathedral. Tudor pub. Souvenir shop. Christian book shop. Antique shop. Second Tudor pub. Shop that sells glass things.

The reason that this sort of thing has been going on for millennia is because the thing people like about towns, right, is that you know where things are and what you're getting. That's why they live in towns. If people wanted a lack of fun places, comforting familiarity and reassuringly branded outlets, they'd live in a swamp.

VILLAGES
∾

Admit it, farmy boy, what's better – a mud-spattered hellhole populated by the same three families for eight million years, many of whom have only reluctantly been persuaded to give up sacrificing cows to the Green Man, and whose local amenities consist of a post office, a smelly shop and a pub full of stranglers, or a lot of exciting media people from London who hold cocaine orgies every night and watch brand-new American TV shows in their thatched Audis on broadband?

Okay, fair point, there isn't much in it, really.

MISCELLANEOUS
OLD CRAP

CATS
~

They're still bastards.

INSECTS
~

At a time when, daily, thousands of species of animal – not thousands of animals, thousands of species – are vanishing from the face of the earth, never to return, it's a bit tactless of scientists to keep reminding us that there are still millions of species of insect left in the world. It seems a bit unfair really. We're short of long-toed reed warblers and feathered crest frogs and African nice hounds and all the rest, but we've still got bugs coming out the wazoo.

Clearly things are not being organized properly. We have a shortage of nice rare animals, and we have a glut of the stingy, buzzy ones. There is an insect surplus and it is not being managed. Could we not come to some sort of arrangement with the animal kingdom? Even the most stubborn of bitey dung beetles would have to agree that things have got out of hand. Perhaps they would be prepared to lose a few million species of fire ant or venomous caterpillar just to let some of the prettier lemurs stick around? But no. Insects just keep on multiplying and flying and buzzing and all we can do is spray them. The unreasonable six-legged bastards.

HONEY
~

Honey is weird for two reasons. One, it looks like some sort of cloudy jam but it's not jam at all, or even marmalade. And two, it's hugely popular but it's actually made from bee spit.

GLASTONBURY

❧

There's no real point talking about other festivals. It's like talking about The Beatles and then going on to mention a lot of Merseyside beat bands. Most so-called 'festivals' aren't festivals at all, they're just rock concerts in fields. And not even proper fields at that; everything at these particular outdoor events is so engineered, so tidy, that

'Up to your ankles in human waste and mud.'

it wouldn't be much of a surprise to discover after the event that the whole thing had taken place on Astroturf in a car park.

But Glastonbury is different. For a start, only a maniac would go there just to see a band. Here's a thing: the band you've just shelled out fourteen thousand pounds to see in a cow pasture is playing tomorrow night, for half the price, in a real room, with a roof on it and walls. It's not windy, so the sound isn't blowing all over the place. It's not raining. The bar is nearby and not gummed up with five hundred weekend crusties. You can go home afterwards. Oh, and you're not up to your ankles in human waste and mud.

And that's just the musical side. Glastonbury is a hellhole. Weak and lazy people compare it to the Somme, which is not only a bit offensive to the people who were actually at the Somme, but also misses the point by a rural mile. Glastonbury is no longer an endurance test with bands. Or, to be more precise, Glastonbury is no longer *just* an endurance test with bands.

Look around you, hypothetical Glasto punter. What do you see? No, not Sting. You see stalls. Millions of stalls. You see mobile-phone companies. You see corporate logos. You see Stella McCartney and her clothes shop. And you see people buying stuff. They may be pelvis-deep in mud, wearing tie-dyed tops, eating something that says it's Mexican but really was boiled up in hell, but they're shopping. Glastonbury is essentially London if it was raining all the time and they forgot to build Oxford Street.

THE NATIONAL TRUST

∾

L ackeys and collaborators, the lot of them. The National Trust, as its name suggests, is meant to be a lovely big looking-after thing where all the beautiful castles and houses and parks in Britain are 'entrusted' to the nation, which will in return pay for their upkeep by subscription and by opening them to a grateful public.

In fact, the National Trust is the teacher's pet of the aristocracy – 'Can I look after your castle, sir? What a lovely estate! We'll be glad to do all the hard work while you sit on a beach in the Maldives drinking cocaine. Of course we'll have to open it to the public! But only once a month. And then just the boring bits.'

'Essentially, the National Trust operates a sort of buy-to-let scheme for toffs.'

Essentially, the National Trust operates a sort of buy-to-let scheme for toffs, where the toff gets his property done up for free, can still live in the nice bits, and allows the rest of us – whose ancestors, by the way, actually built the sodding thing, because when Lord Titsausagey says, 'Yes, my great-grandfather built the East Wing,' he doesn't mean the old gouty soak actually got down there with a cement mixer and a trowel, he means he got someone else to do it, on a wage of sixpence a decade – to have a quick look round once a month between the hours of noon and one minute past noon.

BRAVE NEW WORLD
❧

You have to feel sorry for Aldous Huxley. The originator of a million extraordinary ideas even before he'd taken acid (see PEOPLE WHO SAY, 'WOW! HAVE YOU BEEN TAKING ACID?'), he's been almost written out of popular culture, largely because people are too lazy to differentiate between his *Brave New World* and George Orwell's *1984*.

This is wrong. So when people say, 'God, cloning! It's so *1984*,' or, 'GM foods are just totally Orwellian,' do this. Grab them by the throat, force them to the ground, and say, 'You don't mean *1984*, you nubbin, you mean *Brave New World*. *This* is *1984*!' and do the boot stomping on a human face forever. All right, wear slippers if you must.

WANTED POSTERS
❧

Do these actually work? It seems unlikely. For a start, there's not many of them about. You don't see them in pubs, or chip shops, or blown up to giant size on the walls of cathedrals. In fact, the only time you do see them is either in the post office, which is about to be closed down because people keep robbing it, or in the local police station. And, frankly, the sort of people who frequent police stations are unlikely to go, 'Why, there's One Thumb Jacko! He's been committing some burglaries here, it says. Here, I'll tell you where he's hiding.'

There is only one use for wanted posters. As comical decoration for your bedroom, to show people how amusing you are, with your name on and a photo of you pretending to scowl, and a caption saying WANTED DEAD OR ALIVE FOR BEING REALLY PISSED!!!! Easily as funny as a fake bullfight poster (see FAKE BULLFIGHT POSTERS).

FAKE BULLFIGHT POSTERS
∾

A moment for contemplation here. While every slightly inebriated bloke on holiday in Spain seems to come home with a poster claiming that they are a famous bullfighter (EL GRANDE MICHAEL JENKINS), it is surely fairly rare for an actual bullfighter to have a poster made that claims they are a drunken pillock from Taunton.

RECTORS
∾

Universities are, to say the least, peculiar places, full of traditions that were mostly made up last week and full of themselves, self-contained city states, little slightly smug academic Gormenghasts. With cheap bars, which is nice. However, the most peculiar thing about universities is that some of them like to elect rectors. Now, rectors are not to be confused with directors. The Rector's Cut of a movie would be rubbish. Then again, so is the Director's Cut as a rule.

These rectors are honorary posts, usually. They are essentially a way of tricking a famous person into coming all the way up to Lancaster or Kirckudbrightshire to give a talk to a load of students. The carrot here is that, for a year, they will be the rector of that college, whose privileges include wearing a big gay hat, drinking a lot of sack and appointing someone else to preside over the University Court. The rector does, however, have no real powers. This is because, as you might suppose, universities are not stupid. It's all very well getting Jude Law up for the night to have a chat and a white wine with the students; it's a completely different barrel of budgies to let him run the actual administration of the college. Similarly, while we all admire the comedy of Johnny Vegas, he might be more than reluctant to come up with a workable budget for 2008.

Rectors, incidentally, are not the same as the rectors they have in churches. Those are real rectors, serious men and women who are directly employed by God himself. You really don't want to mess with them.

FLAGS
∾

Flags are very odd. People have very different attitudes to them. Here we wear them and think we are being 60s and cool, or 90s and cool, we're not quite sure (see THE BRITISH FLAG). In America, people wear them and get all teary at Old Glory (see THE AMERICAN FLAG). In other countries, people just squint up at flagpoles and go, 'Is THAT our flag? It's ridiculous.'

The problem with flags is that, as they were often invented before people could read and write, their symbolism can be a bit vague. Some crosses? Some stripes? They look more like semaphore than national emblems. In an ideal world, flags would be like Top Trumps cards. Instead of pictures and shapes, they'd have statistics about how great and powerful each country was. Then, instead of wars, nations would just take their flags to the battlefield and play Top Trumps. 'Hmm, you have a smaller GDP than us ... but more tanks. Damn!'

THE BRITISH FLAG
∾

A symbol of union, and a bloody confusing one. The diagonals are all done at special angles, making it easy to identify spies, who always fly it upside down. The overlay of saints' crosses is very much in England's favour, with Saint Andrew and the other one standing behind trying to get in shot. And where's Wales? They might be 'only' a principality but they're clearly an actual country. So the only explanation for their absence must be that the man who first drew the flag couldn't do dragons.

THE AMERICAN FLAG
~

A symbol of liberty that we're not allowed to take the piss out of, or burn, or cut into tea-towels. Pretty useless symbol of liberty, then (see also THE CONFEDERATE FLAG).

THE CONFEDERATE FLAG
~

Which would have been the flag on every hippy's backside had the bad guys, sorry, the South, won the American Civil War. But they didn't. They lost. And now their flag is being banned in lots of places in the South, for being as bad as the swastika. Several people have taken umbrage at this, on the grounds that it's just the emblem of a proud people, and not Nazi at all. No, just a big old banner that might as well say 'SLAVERY WELCOMED HERE'.

ALL THE OTHER FLAGS IN THE WORLD
~

Are either uninspired copies of the French flag, or bits of the old Soviet flag. The rest are just mental. A duck and a rabbit holding hands? Why not! Some slippers on a plate? Our national dish!

'SHAN'T'
~

Not a word you hear any more. Shame, really.

'GAY'

∼

Much of the dullness in the world was created by lamp-headed pedant daddies going round in the 1970s and 80s complaining that we had been 'robbed' of a useful word, that word being 'gay', once meaning sort of bright and cheerful, and now meaning 'enjoying sex with men'. In fact, the old use of gay was pretty much on the way out, if it had ever been in: very few of us apart from the writers of the *Flintstones* theme having ever had a gay old time. So the new use of 'gay' quite arguably saved the word from extinction.

Weirdly, though, we now have a situation where this latter meaning of 'gay' has itself been perverted, to mean 'crap'. Thus, when a schoolboy tells another schoolboy that his guitar-playing is gay, he is not saying that playing the guitar is something that homosexuals do, he is saying that his friend is crap at playing the guitar.

Whether or not all the lamp-headed pedant daddies will start complaining about this corruption of a perfectly good 80s word for 'man shagging' remains to be seen.

TELEGRAMS FROM THE QUEEN

∼

Telegrams from the Queen – or telemessages, or whatever they're called, it doesn't really matter – are a lovely idea. You reach the age of 100 and the Queen sends you a congratulatory telegram. It's a nice idea and better than getting another book about World War I. But surely at that time of life you'd rather have a bit of peace and quiet, and not be disturbed by publicity-crazed royals firing off telegrams every five seconds. It might be nicer if the Queen just anonymously sent you some jam.

TELEGRAMS FROM THE QUEEN 2

∼

And besides, when you're older you are less likely to be excited about getting a telegram from the Queen. After all, you're older than her. You may have met her several times. You've probably been out with one of her uncles. And so on. Frankly, God bless her, but the Queen is less of a thrill when you're a centenarian.

No, the people who'd really appreciate a telegram from the Queen are generally kids. Between the ages of four – when a child has some grasp of the whole concept of monarchy – and ten – when royalty start to seem a bit uncool – children are very excited about anything regal (and probably believe that the Duchess of York lived on a rock with a dragon, but that's not relevant here).

So why not scrap the whole 100 bit and get the Queen to send a telegram to everyone who's turned five? They'd be really chuffed.

BIRTHDAY PARTIES

∾

Always disappointing. When you're a little kid, you have no control over them at all, and find yourself a spectator at your own party, as your parents announce, 'Now we're going to play a game,' and, 'Now it's time for the cake!' and, 'Now Jimmy is going home because he's ruined everything and his trousers.' You feel paralysed and distant as people give you things – if you're lucky – or hit you – if you're not. This is probably the real reason that kids cry at their own birthday parties. They're not overwhelmed or tired, they're just really angry about being kept out of the loop.

As time goes on, birthday parties do not get any better. All teenage parties are awful as they are predicated on two facts. One, you really really want to have sex. And two, you have no idea how to get any sex. This is generally the point at which most teenagers discover alcohol, so they can stand at the back of the room swigging and trying to look okay about it as the school bastard gets off with the girl of their dreams. The same applies to student parties, only more so, and there's always the frisson that you might be asked to leave after you put a chamberpot on over your underpants, or similar.

The rest just gets grimmer. Thirties, forties, fifties – just a long line of markers where people come up and give you cards that might as well say, 'LOOK! HERE COMES YOUR IMMINENT DEATH!' And then before you know it, you're in a room full of people with walking frames and some nurses you've never met are singing 'Happy Birthday' and, once again, saying, 'Now it's time for the cake!'

And the Queen has two of the bloody things. You'd think she'd be a bit less keen to send all those telegrams out (see TELEGRAMS FROM THE QUEEN).

INVITATIONS
∾

You can't win. Send them out the day before your party and people can't come. Send them out months before and people forget and lose them and six years later say, 'Have you had your party yet?'

INVITATIONS 2
∾

And receiving them is even worse. 'R.S.V.P.' That's just rude. What, you're inviting someone to a party and now you're harassing them to see if they're going to come? It all seems a bit insecure:

'Please come to my party.'
'Okay, ta!'
'So … are you coming to my party?'
'I think so.'
'YOU HAVE TO TELL ME NOW YES OR NO!'
'Well, can I check my diary first?'
'YES OR NO! YES OR NO!'

Fun for none of the family.

DEVELOPING COUNTRIES
∾

A phrase introduced to avoid the ranking-system stigma of the 'Third World'. After all, being a so-called Third World country is a bit like being in the Third Division, except you might have more money for boots. 'Developing countries' is a pleasant replacement, implying as it does that some poor sod of a country is in fact on the way up, rather than sweating under the iron heels of famine, drought, war and debt (presumably these heels are being worn by some sort of quadruped, like an iron cow).

Well, good. But surely it's also going to make people in what we used to call the First World a bit edgy. Are we saying that countries like Britain, France and that little one under Belgium are in fact NOT developing? Are we the 'declining countries'? Because that's the kind of loose talk that starts trouble. So watch it.

REACTOLITE GLASSES
∾

Designed to eliminate the need for sunglasses, reactolite glasses and their ilk in fact never quite succeed. This is because when you come in from the sunny outside to indoorland, the change from SUNGLASSES MODE to INDOOR MODE is never quite complete, and your friends are looking at someone who apparently likes looking slightly, but not too much, like a crazed dictator. Meanwhile, from your side of the specs, everything is a weird sort of 1970s brown.

POSH CHARITY SHOPS
∾

Long, long ago, when charity shops were devoted solely to making money to give to poor and sick people, they were great. Everything was cheap. The cheap and nasty stuff was cheap, the really crap stuff was cheap, the reasonable stuff was cheap – and the brilliant stuff was cheap. It was a genuine democracy. For every dubious old cheesegrater or used tie, there was a really interesting book or an astonishingly rare record. And they were all dirt cheap.

These days, many charity shops seem to have decided to get with it and live in the 'real world' (see LIVING IN THE REAL WORLD). They have confused themselves with real shops and would, if pressed, tell you about marketing and overheads and stuff like they were a megastore or something. And so, slowly and cruelly, they have drained the fun out of going into charity shops.

All the crap has gone. This is not only silly, but annoying. There are still people who a) really want an egg-slicer, and b) have only got ten pence to spend on one. All the really bad clothes have gone. This is bad, because up-and-coming indie bands and designers need really bad clothes, to put on their skinny frames and make the rest of us want those clothes too.

Second to worst of all is the Ownbrand products. These are supplied exclusively to this chain of charity shops and you can see why. They are new-age bollocks of the worst kind. Scented candles. Wicker pot-holders. Incense. Glass coasters. Little pretend diamondy things that hang on a thread. The people in developing countries (see DEVELOPING COUNTRIES) who make this stuff must think that we're all mental. And they'd be right.

But worst of all is that charity shops have now wised up to the bargain thing. They've noticed that people were buying things cheaply in their stores that were going for vast amounts of money elsewhere. And they've put their prices up, thereby not only removing what was unique, charming and even exciting about charity shops, but also ensuring that everybody goes on eBay instead, where it's cheaper (see INTERNET AUCTIONS).

YOU CAN'T OPEN A NEWSPAPER THESE DAYS WITHOUT …

~

Another thing that people only say who write columns. The only thing you actually can't open a newspaper these days without doing is reading an article that doesn't contain the phrase, *'You can't open a newspaper these days without …'*

BANANAS DURING THE WAR

~

A small thing. People who grew up during World War II are forever telling people who didn't that, 'We never saw a banana during the War.' Now, while this is probably almost certainly true, it raises a couple of issues. Surely there were other things you never saw during the War? Fry's Turkish Delight, for example. Vodka Martinis. Chicken tikka masala. Why pick on bananas? And, while we're on the subject, so what? Very few people want to see a banana anyway. They're just not that interesting.

Maybe people were just upset because practical jokes were very popular during World War II and the banana shortage meant that there was no banana peel for fat comedy shopkeepers to slip on. But it seems unlikely.

LEAVING YOUR FRONT DOOR OPEN

It never seems to occur to elderly Cockney and Northern folk, most of whom are wearing a pinny and shaking their heads sadly when they come out with this honking great yawnigram, that there are good reasons why 'in the old days you could leave your front door open and nobody would come in'. One is that nobody came in because they didn't want to have their heads bored off their own necks, and two, because in those days nobody had anything worth nicking.

BEING GOOD TO THEIR MOTHERS

Yes, in them days, psychotic killers masquerading as rogues-cum-community spokespersons were indeed famous for 'being good to their mothers'. But this fact is slightly less impressive when one considers that they went round killing everyone else. Presumably the reason they were good to their mothers was that there was then some-one to cook their tea for them when they got home from a hard day's murdering.

'POLITICAL CORRECTNESS GONE MAD'

Odd how all the people who throw down their *Daily Madbastard* in disgust and shout, 'It's political correctness gone mad!' never throw up their arms in delight when they hear some example of polit-ical correctness gone sane. But then, having some racist knobstone thrown out of a reality show, or building a wheelchair access ramp, or, you know, just abolishing slavery is not only not as much fun as stories about kids not allowed to bring conkers to a Nativity play or whatever, they're also less … made-up. And fiction is always more fun than fact.

'BUT NOT IN A GOOD WAY'

A modern comedy cliché, used like this: 'It was disgusting and wet. But not in a good way.' This phrase is the modern equivalent of the 70s tag 'And that was just the girls' and should be avoided. Until about 2020, when it will be ironic again for about three weeks.

RELIGION

Ignoring all the business about if it's true or not (and of course, dear reader, your particular faith is the best one), it's great, isn't it, how we still need religion to guide our lives and direct our morality? Like we're all seven years old. Religion should be like stabilisers on a bike; useful when you're learning how to do stuff, and then something to take off and put in the garage when you've got the hang of things.

Anyone who can't tell good from bad and right from wrong without a) a list of crimes, and b) a list of threats, shouldn't be allowed out of the house. And anyone who can doesn't need someone in a frock (cheap shot) to tell them what to do. Unless, of course, it's a very nice frock.

FEAR

The world is being run on fear at the moment. Every time something appalling happens, we all get more scared. Or at least we are all encouraged to get more scared. Once upon a time our leaders used to say things like, 'We have nothing to fear but fear itself.' Now they say things like, 'Everyone be really scared forever.' The fact that it's easier to run the world when everyone is absolutely terrified has nothing to do with it, of course.